Dear Reader
I'm Jo, a
and I ho;
Dolly's bittersweet festive
tale set in fictional
Wakeley, Yorkshire

The Fifty Lost Christmases of Dolly Hunter

(first Edition)

Jo Priestley

If you could spare the time to leave a rating or a review on Amazon, I would be extremely grateful to you.

First published September 2023
Copyright © Jo Priestley
All rights reserved.

Best wishes from Jo.

Other titles in the Women of Old Yorkshire series

The Calling of Highbrook
The Strangers in Me
Little Robin
Orla Metcalfe Has Run Away
Delfina

Dedication

Dolly Hunter is very dear to my heart. I wrote this story four years ago but have waited until 2023 to publish, as this marks fifty years since my village faced adversity. This book is my tribute to the kindness and the mettle of the people in my community I grew up with and was lucky enough to know.

I was always destined to write a Christmas tale one day. I'm the person who plans for the big day all year and counts down the days to September when I can really throw myself into preparation without seeming odd. I was keen however to write a tale with many layers to the plot, so it wasn't purely about Christmas alone. It took me a year to plan and a year to write, and it is the book which has given me the most pleasure and satisfaction throughout the whole writing process.

Thanks again to Andrew for editing my sixth book this year -I think he deserves a rest for a while—and to Megan for adapting the cover from original artwork by Hansuan Fabregas; to my local farm shop, for stocking my entire range of books, and to the staff there who read the books themselves and cheer me on; and to (in alphabetical order) Ann, Janet, Sue and Tracey, my reviewers, who make me believe in my writing ability when I wonder if I'll be one of the 95% of authors who sell less than one hundred copies of their book in their lifetime.

Then again, making one hundred people happy is no small thing and I'll happily settle for that.

Chapter 1
Dolly Now

For me it's soothing, like slipping into a warm bath when you're cold to the bone, or the cusp between consciousness and a solid night's sleep.

When my life was in turmoil it was elusive, and I yearned for it. I find there's certainty and security to be found in routine and the comfort it brings. Some may think me dull, people crave excitement nowadays, but that doesn't bother me.

Our row's not as high and mighty as it used to be but like my mother told me often, standards must be upheld. The creep of decay will soon take hold if you don't keep your eye on it, she warned me. Chipboard covers the holes where the windows once sat on some houses. They stand like plasters on a wound, but Saturday mornings still find me fettling my own windows in the same way she did, week after week, year after year. I think of her every time.

Already, the clouds are hanging low, yet its barely mid-September. The smoke from the first fires of autumn billow in and around the skeletal hats of the houses further down the row. I've watched them lose their grimy black tiles one by one over decades. Each one that drops and shatters fills me with a sense of foreboding, but I refuse to dwell on it. Our row has fared better, with only two out of the six houses now standing empty, yet mercifully intact.

The familiar smoky aroma makes me keen to get my own fire going. I'm settled by the sight of a hefty sack of coal, so I stock up in summer when it's cheaper. Winter may spread out long and dark before us each year, but a roaring fire gives me my greatest pleasure of an evening. That and of course the telly. I find the comfort of routine is all the better because I lived with a knot in my stomach for years. Because I was hungry and deprived, even when the larder was crammed with food. By rights I should have wanted for nothing.

The sound of a van gets steadily louder, and I wait for it to stop outside my front gate as usual. I know without looking it's Frank with his bread. He tells me I'm his best customer, so he makes me his first port of call each week. I want to make it worth his while to keep coming, so I buy for the week and bob it in the little freezer in the cellar. You'll get anything from a carpet tack to a 13-amp fuse and all the food imaginable you can squeeze in a tin from Sally Evans's, but her stodgy bread and baps aren't fit for the birds.

Frank's early mind. Perhaps he's got something on later and wants to get his round done and dusted. Pulling my sleeves down I rub my damp hands quickly over my work trousers to dry them. I glance over my shoulder as I head back up the steps to nip inside for my purse.

Pausing halfway I realise it's not Frank after all; in fact, I don't even recognise the van. Who's having visitors at this hour, I wonder. Who's having visitors at all? The mist is thinning but I still can't see who's in there for the tall reflection of the houses on the windscreen. I squint, my eyes following the van, and I notice in my peripheral the ghostly outline of Mrs Turrell next door peering from behind her nets. She's a nosy old beggar that one, but you won't find me complaining.

The van looks to be slowing down now. I've swiftly moved over the threshold and out of sight, but I carefully place one foot on the highest of the four steps, nudging my head out just enough. The van comes to a halt at the end of the row, in front of the house next to Ralph's. That can't be right surely, number twenty-three has stood empty for years since Robert and Esther left. I quickly try and calculate how long exactly. I can't remember, which says a lot, but Ralph's made sure he's looked after it through necessity as much as sentimentality with the house being right next door to him.

I'm agitated, keen to continue the flow of my morning, but I'm somehow unable to move until I satisfy myself who it is. I wait and stay exactly in position. The engine turns off, but nobody appears, and now I can't help blowing out my impatience. I've too many tasks to get through this morning for a disruption to my routine.

The passenger door slamming makes me jump, even though I'm expecting it. Pulling my neck in instinctively to limit the risk of being seen, I still need to wait a second or two longer.

Finally, two figures appear from behind the van, slowly coming into focus through the smoggy haze of the morning. I see a woman holding the hand of a small girl. They're not from round here, I can tell immediately just by looking at them. The woman has a thick auburn horse's mane ponytail hanging over her shoulders; she's wearing jeans and what looks like fine leather boots, with a nice-looking bag slung across her body. The girl is small but maybe older than she looks, with blonde curls springing from her ponytail on the crown of her head. I recognise the colours of the football shirt she's wearing but I've never in my life seen a girl wearing one.

I watch them standing side by side to look up at the house together. They stare at the tired old place for the longest time like it's the loveliest sight they've ever seen. I'm entranced as the woman now smiles down at her daughter. I just know it's her daughter… it's the smile of a mother. The same way my mother smiled at me.

I'm taken aback when the woman suddenly looks up in the direction of my door. I pull my head in slightly even though I'm convinced I'm well out of sight.

But then I see her smile widen so she shows me the whites of her teeth. The sight somehow startles me. She lifts her hand and waves right in my direction.

What the… I back myself inside, more than a little alarmed, then slam the door hurriedly so the letterbox rattles. I'm breathing heavily. The brass neck of that one, I think. This Saturday morning has just turned very peculiar.

I can't altogether say I like it much.

*

Pausing mid-bite of a beef and onion sandwich, I see a familiar outline rush past the window through the net curtains. Ralph's on his way over already by the look of it. That's odd because I can ordinarily set my watch by him. Only a handful of us bother nowadays even for the harvest festival but we try and make it count. Now I feel the need to hurry my lunch and guzzle down the dregs of my tea because I'm playing catchup. Banking the fire I put the guard over, so it won't take long to get it going again when I get back. A chilly house is a dismal home and I'll not have that.

I rise on tiptoes to look in the mottled mirror over the mantle. Patting my hair, though I take great pains to ensure it never moves much, I agitatedly apply lipstick. I found the perfect shade of *Toffee Caramel* when I was seventeen and stuck with it. I'm not really one for too much makeup other than a dab of powder, but I could *never* leave the house with naked lips for some reason. I clip on my mother's favourite earrings as usual but I've no time to check today if they're on straight. Sliding into my long camel coat I head through the kitchen and out the back door, cursing Ralph for giving me that irksome little sensation of being rushed. He knows better than anyone how I hate that feeling.

On my way across the road to the woods, I turn my head right then left. It's a pointless act as traffic is almost defunct round here and I can hear well enough; but I observe the ritual anyway. The imposing building looms as large and dead as ever above the houses. It's a daily reminder in more ways than one. I thought I'd get used to seeing it after a while, like a scar you can't take your eyes off to start with and then never notice over time.

Yet it didn't happen.

I walk only thirty seconds or so through the trees. They're still in the full bloom of summer for now so the little green tin church seems to appear out of nowhere. By, it's a beauty. Thomas Worthington did Wakeley a huge favour when he had it made as a prefab back in 1875. It was only supposed to be a temporary place for the copperworkers- or the c'workers as we've always called them - and their families to gather, but it's had so much tender loving care heaped on it over the years that it's become a mainstay. I'm one of two who provide the tender loving care currently and I'll continue to do so as long as there's breath in my body. When I stand with my back to the road to look at it as I often do, I can pretend I'm in another world. I'm glad of that feeling sometimes.

If I'm honest, the building means more to me than the significance of it really, but my mother told me years ago to keep that little revelation to myself.

"Everybody doesn't need to know everything about you, Dolly," she said when I told her once, "especially when your thoughts might be a touch controversial."

I've taken her advice about that and many things.

"Well, hello Dolly," Ralph gives me his regular greeting mimicking the line from the song and finding himself very funny.

Age is a great leveller I think, noting the tatty tendrils of his ice white hair. It's a shame the once best-looking lad in Wakeley has almost gone. Almost, but not quite; he still scrubs up nicely on a church day, but he's always far too busy to be bothered with all that. I never like to get too close to his overalls because I can tell they've never seen the inside of a washing machine.

"You're keen," I tell him, "I hadn't even got my sandwich down when I saw you passing the window."

I sound irritated because I am.

"I know but I told the young lass that's moved in next door that I'd give her a hand putting her beds up later. She said she could manage but I can't see her struggling. I expect you saw the van earlier."

The twinkle in his eye tells me my peeping tom act didn't go unnoticed when the van arrived. I brush it off. I want to know what he already knows but I'll not give him the satisfaction of asking. Never one to use one word when two will do is our Ralph so I don't have to wait long to find out.

"Her name's Harriet. She's from Leeds and she's taken a job at the town hall as a clerk. Her daughter, Lydia is seven. Lovely little thing, never stops smiling, just like her mother."

By the doe-eyed expression on his face, it looks like the two of them have made quite an impression already. He didn't let the grass grow.

"No husband then?" I sniff, searching for something in his eyes.

"Give me chance, Doll, I only had time for a five-minute chat."

He smiles, looking down quickly and fiddling with the dirty string holding his spade handle together. I've no use for mine so I'll pass it on I think, because he'll not buy a new one. The rosy hue slowly colouring his cheeks somehow tweaks my tetchiness.

"The town hall, you say, I can't imagine there's much call for an extra clerk there. The place is dying on its feet as far as I can tell," I say, my tone deceptively level.

Why come to live in Wakeley I wonder, it's not exactly the peoples' choice; not nowadays.

"She might have said personal assistant, but it all amounts to the same, shuffling papers. Bernie must need an extra pair of hands to keep his head above water. I often think he'll be on his way before long like the rest of them. I can't imagine the town hall without Bernie. It'd be like *No.10* without the prime minister."

A guffaw escapes me at the ludicrous comparison.

"Hardly, but I for one don't want to have to pay my rates in Thorndale, it's a right trek, especially with the winter bus service."

We fall silent with our unspoken thoughts for a moment. So subtle it barely registered at first but little by little we've had to adjust to managing with less. Less people, less amenities, less of the everyday. It jogs my memory, shaking my mind out of the mire.

"While I think on, the vicar's seventieth is coming up and I thought about having a collection. We need him on side as long as possible because when he retires, they'll not replace him, not with a full-time vicar at least."

"Leave it with me," he says, pulling his tiny notebook and pencil out of his top pocket.

"Thanks. So, the new lass will have her work cut out doing up Robert's old place after all this time," I say. I can't help fishing for more information, it's not often we see a new face nowadays.

"It's not so bad inside. Jonny asked me to give it a once-over on Wednesday when he told me they were moving in. He's known for a couple of weeks but never got round to telling me; you know what he's like. In any case, it's more than liveable for the time being and you know I've always looked after the bones of the place. I imagine she'll give it a lick of paint throughout to begin with. I might give her a hand if she likes."

I'm barely listening.

"You've known since Wednesday they were coming, why didn't you tell me?"

"I haven't seen you so I'm telling you now."

The back of my neck starts prickling. That's enough.

"Don't you get clever with me, Ralph Kellett," I snap.

His eyes widen as I turn on my heel to go inside. I've extra to do to set up for tomorrow and it's better for both of us if I bid a hasty retreat. On my way in, I touch the unassuming brass plaque under the lamp next to the door as always. It's the last thing to polish before I leave. I take my time and find quiet satisfaction in watching the shine restored for another week.

I sense a gentle change from one atmosphere to another by simply crossing a threshold. The silence smooths my ruffled feathers as I make my way into the back room for the cleaning paraphernalia and trestle table. The leather pew seats still need a good waxing even if only a few will be taken.

Hopeful of the usual donations I place the table for the baskets at the front of the altar then iron the blue and white cotton tablecloth over the surface with my hands. The flowery pattern is on its way to being washed away forever, but it's serviceable enough.

I can't help but smile to myself in the stillness of the church.

That Ralph, I think. He winds me off the clock but it's strange how significant he's been in my life. How he was the one who finally unlocked my door to a new kind of happiness.

Yet the old boy still hasn't got a clue.

Chapter 2

I don't go so far as wearing a hat for church like my mother, but I do have three best outfits I like to wear on rotation.

Today it's the turn of my navy shift dress and powder blue jacket. Navy shoes and handbag finish me off nicely. According to the magazines, matching accessories aren't the thing any longer, but I'm not bohemian enough to mess about mismatching. My weight doesn't fluctuate much, and that suits me because I can get plenty of wear out of my clothes. They're well looked after and good as new so who cares if they've seen me wearing them umpteen times before. Who takes any notice of a middle-aged woman anyway? If I'm honest I probably look a little bit older than those I've seen of similar years on the telly, but like Ralph, I haven't the money, time, or inclination to worry about life's fripperies.

Half past nine is a late start for me, although I've done plenty already. I'm up at half past five in the week to get the cleaning under my belt at Langley's because it's a bit of a walk. The dairy is about the only place to work now for those of us left who aren't retired. I was in the office for years but then I took over from my mother doing the cleaning there after she died. It was a relief as things were always changing in the office with technology and such, so I was well shut of the stress. Me and mam bought our house years ago from the landlord, Jonny Pritchard, so I can get by nicely if I add on the wage from cleaning the vicarage and doing the vicar's shopping. That's another reason why I want to hang on to him. Maybe that's selfish on my part but a little self-preservation never harmed anyone.

I see Ralph pass the window as I'm putting on my lipstick. He's not on his own I notice. I better get a move on. Blast that man, that's twice in as many days he's had me on the back foot.

I can feel a mood coming on. I slam the back door harder than I need to, but it doesn't make me feel any better.

Looking left as I cross the road, I see my nemesis, but I haven't time to give it any more thought for once. I take some deep breaths as I walk through the woods to the church. I want to arrive in my usual serene state despite Ralph's best efforts to upend them. As I touch the brass plaque, I notice he's sitting down already with the newcomers by his side and a spare seat on his other waiting for me. The vicar's fussing with the layout of the table and reading the handwritten tags on the baskets of food. I call them baskets but nowadays they're cardboard boxes covered in wrapping paper or occasionally tin foil with some kind of bow added for decoration. There's a slightly bigger turn out than usual I notice, and a fancy-looking proper basket in the centre of the display. I know everyone by name and swiftly acknowledge them with a nod as I head up the aisle.

Ralph nudges over as I sit down. I can see two sets of the same-coloured eyes on the other side of him staring and they're smiling at me again. He's right, they don't stop smiling but it's making me uncomfortable. I give another quick little nod now in their direction and look ahead towards the altar.

"Good turn-out," Ralph whispers, "Dolly, this is…"

His introductions are interrupted when the vicar starts the service, so I don't have to acknowledge the three of them. I'm relieved as my mood's not shifting.

The vicar's overbearing voice sounds far away for once. I can't take my eyes off the big basket on the trestle table. Some might call it garish, but I must remember it's not for me, it's for the elderly.

Those who don't put in an appearance for the service still drop off donations all Saturday afternoon after I've left and then early on the Sunday morning. Sally Evans must do a bomb in her shop this time of year.

I keep my eyes fixed firmly ahead, even though I'm keen to give the newcomers a look over. I'm trying to pull my mind back to the service, but it still wanders to the woman and child throughout. I can sense their presence to my core.

Ralph shuffles beside me, and I hear the vicar thanking us for attending and donating, so I know the service is drawing to a close. I fiddle inside my handbag for a tissue for something to do to take my mind off the impending introductions. I must soon make polite conversation and small talk with the two strangers. Ralph nudges me so I have no option but to get up and make my way outside.

The vicar greets us all in turn and shakes our hands.

"Thank you for coming," he says each time.

It would wear me out. I stand at the side of the gate, and everyone has a quick word as they're passing. Ralph and his company wait patiently, then I see them heading my way when they see the opportunity. I quickly take in the sight of a well-turned-out mother and daughter. The mother's hair is in a smart bun and the daughter is wearing a dress. Thank heavens for small mercies, I think, not a football shirt in sight.

Ralph's hopping about, chomping at the bit to make the introductions, and not hiding it well.

"Dolly, this is Harriet and Miss Lydia. Harriet and Miss Lydia, this is Dolly," he says.

Dolly. Dolly! Miss Hunter if you please Ralph, I think, but I can't say it. They're both looking at me in such a way I'm finding it impossible to meet their eyes.

The bairn speaks first.

"Mr Ralph lets me call him Mr Ralph," she says, "please may I call you Mrs Dolly?"

My mouth opens and closes. I suppose it's a step up from the first option, but I can't help but correct her.

"Miss Dolly will be fine," I tell her, shaking her outstretched hand. Impeccable manners I see even if she is a bit precocious.

Her mother looks my way beaming and offers her own hand.

"I'm very pleased to meet you, Miss Dolly," she says.

It's as though she's having a look into my soul, and I shiver a little. I turn my mouth up at the edges slightly and shake her soft, warm hand. Dropping my eyes from the scrutiny a shiver runs through me once more.

"Well then, there we are," Ralph says, grinning like he's lost his mind. It's catching by the looks of it. He starts to babble in a way I've never heard him before.

"So, Harriet and Lydia are from Leeds and she's going to work at the town hall," he says animatedly.

"Yes, I remember you telling me yesterday," I tell him a touch sharply, but he doesn't notice.

Has the man taken leave of his senses? I decide it might be best to waylay him.

"I know it's early days, but do you like the house? Only the best would do for Robert and Esther Hargreaves, so hopefully it's still in a good enough condition to be comfortable," I ask Harriet.

"It feels like home already," she says, "and Ralph insists he'd like to give me a hand with one or two jobs."

She smiles over the bairn's head at him, and he smiles back. I'm shocked—he's older than me and it looks like he's got some sort of crush on her. Oh, for goodness' sake.

I'm glad for the bairn to break the silence.

"Mr Ralph is going to play football with me on an afternoon. I play in goal so he's going to kick the football into my net so I can practice."

"I'm going to try, but I think you'll be hard to get past, judging by earlier this morning."

She giggles and he ruffles the curls on her head. Well, here's a fine to-do I think, they've just met and are acting like old friends.

"What about school?" I ask, bringing us back into the real world.

"There's a vacancy at Thorndale Primary from January so it's been agreed I can home school Lydia on a morning and then work afternoons until then." Harriet tells me, levelly.

She smiles all the time she speaks, her eyes never leaving mine.

I sniff, embarrassed.

"I'm impressed. So much done in one day."

My voice sounds tart even to me, but she doesn't seem fazed.

"I've been busy with telephone calls and on-line form-filling and such," she says sweetly, "but I like to plan ahead."

She laughs and I instinctively accompany her with a small fake one.

"While I think on," she says, "I took the liberty of contributing to the Harvest Festival table with one or two things, I hope you don't mind. We can give you and Ralph a hand delivering the food if you think it would help."

"That's very kind of you but we have our little routine, and we soon whip around the houses."

I'm uncomfortable, hot even as I wave and throw a tight smile at the vicar on his way past.

"I say all hands to the pump," Ralph grins.

Oh, I bet you do, mister, I think.

"It'll give them chance to meet some of the townsfolk, Dolly. It's hard moving somewhere new when you don't know anyone."

Well, he should know, I think. He disappeared without trace for long enough after what happened. But it looks like I'm beaten. All three faces are tilted my way, waiting for authorisation. I cough daintily behind my hand.

"Very well, I'll meet you back here in half an hour after I've changed my shoes."

"We'll come with you. It won't take you two minutes," Ralph says breezily.

My arm's so far up my back, he'll snap it in two if he's not careful.

Staring back at the three smiling faces, I want to run for the hills and hide.

*

As I unlock the door, I still sense all eyes upon my back, burning holes in my best powder blue jacket. There's a big part of me which wants to shut the door in their face and have them standing there while I change my shoes. But

I can hear my mother's voice saying, "Manners maketh man and woman, Dolly," so I bite the bullet.

Standing with the door in my hand I invite them inside my kitchen, telling them not to bother taking their shoes off. Ralph looks taken aback but I don't want to hang about and it's dry enough outside.

They follow him into the front room.

"Do sit down," I say from the back.

My voice sounds like the queen inviting the prime minister to take a seat for the first time in her parlour or wherever it is they meet.

"Oh, it's so pretty in here, Mrs Dolly," says Lydia, "my grandpa has a clock like that. Does it chime every hour like his?"

"Miss Dolly," I correct her, thinking what on earth came over Ralph to agree to these ludicrous new titles, "yes it does, in fact."

"It is a very lovely room," Harriet confirms, "I much prefer old things to new."

She's buttering me up. Old things do not appeal to the young 'uns. They like shiny, new, and expensive and when they stop working, they just throw them away instead of mending them.

I'm proud of my front room mind and I'm warmed by a little glow of something. Perhaps pride, but then they say pride comes before a fall and I'm not daft enough to fall for it.

I pull my shoes from the cupboard under the stairs, thinking I could just settle down with a cup of tea right now. I lace up my shoes quickly. They're navy, so I'll still look fairly presentable, and I can't help listening in as they continue chatting amongst themselves.

"So, what time do you start work on an afternoon?" Ralph asks Harriet.

"One," she responds, "so I'll have to continue home school when I get back. Are you sure you don't mind watching Lydia for me for the time being, Ralph? I do have the number of a registered childminder the school gave me who's not too far away."

"It would be a pleasure," he says, "I need to get fitter anyway and no doubt she'll keep me on my toes."

They all laugh together, even though I suspect the bairn has no idea what he's talking about. I stand up straight again thinking that Ralph's getting on my nerves, he doesn't even sound like himself.

"She's definitely taken a shine to you in such a short space of time, that's for sure," Harriet tells him, looking down at her daughter.

I can fair see his chest puff up under his jacket. There's no fool like an old fool, I know that much.

"Ready," I say.

I must have said it a bit louder than intended because they all spin their startled faces in my direction and there's not a smile in sight for once.

Jumping up in unison they follow me to the back door.

Let me get out of here, I think, flicking down the yale lock and banging the door clumsily behind me. I'm red hot and not just from the fire.

I need some space to breathe.

Chapter 3
Dolly Then

I'm best friends with Margaret, our dads are best friends and so were our grans. You can't fake a feeling, it's either right or it's not. Margaret is the best friend anyone could wish for and I'm glad she picked me.

They're not here anymore which is sad but Margaret and me, loved to hear our grans telling us tales of our dads. They called them the 'naughty nippers' because they got up to all sorts. Nothing horrible mind, just funny. Mam used to call our grans a right couple of characters. I was called after mine, but we couldn't have two Dorothy's so that's why they called me Dolly. I like Dolly anyway because I don't know anyone else who's called it, not in Wakeley at least.

Margaret's always been poorly but you never hear her moan about it. She's quite frail and thin and mam says she's got a bad heart. I always think this sounds odd when she's got such a good heart. She gets picked up to go on the long trip to the Infirmary in Leeds once a month for a check-up and she's waiting for an operation when her hearts as big as it will grow. I think that's what mam said. The last year she's been on bed rest, so I call and see her every night after tea and for most of Saturday and Sunday afternoons. Margaret worries it's too much, but I just tell her I wouldn't want to be anywhere else. When I'm not with her, it's strange because I wish I was. She does a bit of schoolwork, but I don't think anybody's bothered, it's just to stop her being bored really. Uncle Robert and my dad saved up for a little second hand black and white telly for her room when they found out about her having to stay in bed, so we watch it together. Margaret picks out what's good to watch from the paper and we've got our regular shows we'd never miss.

I'm back at school after the summer holidays. It was a bit colder than it usually is in August and we had more rain, so I was glad we didn't miss out on too much sunshine for once. It would have been hard for both of us listening to kids playing in the street and in their back yards. Especially for Margaret.

"I'd be surprised if you don't get at least six O-levels," Margaret says, propped in bed with her hair freshly washed and blow dried. I help her mam to wash it once a week.

I think I might even get seven if I'm lucky, but I keep it to myself as I don't want to sound like a bragger. I passed my eleven-plus so I could have gone to Thorndale Grammar School. Mam and dad thought the secondary modern would be better for a girl. and anyway, all my friends were set to go there. Qualifications are all well and good, but options are limited around here and I'm not moving away, not ever, so that's that.

I miss Margaret not being at school and the bus rides aren't the same. We always had plenty to talk about and the time flew by. She always called for me so we could walk to the bus stop together. It's the little things like that I miss most.

I tell Margaret often there's plenty of reasons I'm jealous of her. Like the shape of her nails, her long neck, her tiny feet, how quietly she talks, but the main thing I'm jealous of is her long, dark, shiny hair. We use the same shampoo but mines still not as shiny as hers. She says it's not that I'm jealous of her, it's that I envy her which is different. That's another thing, she thinks very deeply and she's very sensible. I often think it's just as well because I'd go stark, staring bonkers if I was laid in bed all day long. I've only stayed in bed once in my whole life with proper flu where I couldn't lift my head off the pillow for a week. Mam says I never go to bed when I'm unwell generally because I'm frightened of missing something.

Margaret tells me she envies my blue eyes, small nose, no-nonsense attitude to life, but most of all my sense of humour. We do have a right laugh and I think this is the main reason why we're such good friends. We're different but the same if that can be true.

I can't believe it's September already. Autumn's the gateway to all things Christmas mam says. I'm excited, knowing the fun we have in front of us for the next three and a half months. That's a whole barrel-load of fun if I think about it.

The Harvest Festival's coming up and we do a box of food to donate like everyone else. You'd be shamed if you didn't, but I like getting things together with mam. That's the first time I really feel like Christmas is around the corner every year.

"Let me guess what Mrs Turrell contributed," Margaret says, that Sunday afternoon when I call round after church, "a tinned steak and kidney pie, a tin of carrots, potatoes and peas, a tub of gravy, a golden syrup sponge pudding and a tin of custard."

I nod and laugh. She's spot on. It used to be fresh fruit and vegetables in the boxes but now it's mainly tins, so that they last longer.

"It'll make somebody a fine dinner," Margaret mimics in her best hoity toity voice just like Mrs Turrell.

Although we find it hilarious, we both agree hers is the best basket. Normally Margaret would do the rounds with me, and we always put it to one side for Ralph's gran, who lives second from the end. We love her to bits.

I never understand why the last three months of the year go by so quickly because January to March is the same amount of time, and it drags on forever. Every day seems exactly the same until the Easter holidays.

We've decided to make bonfire night extra special this year, to give Margaret something nice to look forward to. We generally light the fireworks and the fire over the other side of the wood so we're going to watch them from her mam and dad's bed at the front of the house. Ralph and his mate, Billy got the younger kids to go chumping for wood for weeks using a set of old shopping trolley wheels with a bit of hardboard fastened on top from my dad's shed which he said we could have. They're only allowed to pick pieces of wood which have fallen from the trees, but people tend to donate old wood they kept by from jobs they've done over the year. Ralph and Billy have started their apprenticeships at *Worthies* now, so they need to build the fire on a Saturday. It's always too late for the younger ones by the time they get home from work and have their tea. I wave my scarf out of the window when Margaret tells me they're stood in the best place for her to see it and that's where they build it.

It turns out to be one of the best nights of my life. Our dads stand either side of the window drinking beer on account of it being Friday night, and our mams join us on the end of the bed to watch the raggedy old Guy start the fire and then the fireworks. I think the boys must have told people about our plan for Margaret because there's more than ever and the fire keeps going for ages longer than usual. I love watching Margaret's face sort of glowing in the dark bedroom. There's always a big turn-out, only the really old people stay home, and the lads deliver them some food, so nobody misses out, ever.

Margaret's mam keeps coming upstairs with pots of tea. Ralph brings over potatoes wrapped in foil from the fire, and my mams brought a stew to put on top, over great dollops of butter. We finish off with the parkin and bonfire toffee I made with mam yesterday. I wonder if everyone in the whole country is eating the same tea as we are in Wakeley.

"By, that didn't touch the sides. Thanks for the feast, ladies," dad says, and we all nod our agreement on account of our teeth being glued together with toffee.

He's brought some beer along and Uncle Robert ribs him about being tight because it's the cheapest Sally Evans sells.

"We're not all rolling in it like you, now you're a big chief at *Worthies*," dad tells him.

Uncle Robert finishes off his toffee and we wait to see what he has to say about it.

"Well, if you know what's good for you, you'll keep your trap shut and not come out with wisecracks like that. I'm the gaffer now, mate."

They both have a laugh together and we join in. Uncle Robert's still the same as he always was. He's not up himself like some of the dads who have been promoted to a foreman in the past.

When we get back home, dad goes up to bed because he's ten sheets to the wind, as mam tells him, and me and mam stay up and have a sherry together. I have it in my small glass with a handle which has a tiny Scotsman in a kilt playing bagpipes on the side. Mam told me last Christmas I was old enough to have a sherry in the house and it's always special because we don't often have one.

I look across at her, sitting by the fire with her legs crossed. She's tall so she's got long legs. I envy them. She's holding a cigarette, with her elbow on the chair arm and I notice she's painted her nails in a pale pink. I like the colour; it must be new for tonight because I haven't seen it in her collection before.

I think about how Margaret's mam isn't like mine. I think about this often for all kinds of reasons.

"Aunt Esther seems a lot older than you," I say.

Mam laughs.

"That came from nowhere," she says, taking a puff of her cigarette and blowing it to one side, "she is a bit older, but she's been cursed with the melancholia, it's a terrible ager. She was a worrier before she had Margaret but now, she's got plenty to worry about. Your Uncle Robert has his work cut out, looking after them both but he just seems to get on with it. Best way I suppose if you can do it."

I think about the time of year and how good it makes me feel.

"Why don't they celebrate Christmas in the way we do?" I ask.

I haven't liked to ask Margaret. I was waiting for her to tell me, but she's probably used to it and doesn't know what she's missing out on. I think about the warm glow it gives you inside on Christmas Day and for weeks before. Mam stubs her cigarette out on the tall ashtray at the side of her chair then empties it into the fire.

"Aunt Esther doesn't celebrate Christmas for her own reasons and her heritage is very important to her, so we must respect that. Robert insists on some celebrating for Margaret's sake but it's a shame how they miss out on the magic."

It is a shame I think, especially this year. Now bonfire nights over, it would be nice for Margaret to have something to look forward to. She really shouldn't miss out on the magic this year and I can sense a plan forming. I must proceed with caution mind, because I'd not want to get on the wrong side of Aunt Esther, and neither would Margaret for that matter.

But I can't help it that when I get an itch I just have to scratch; some things are just impossible to ignore.

Chapter 4

Me and mam like to make an early start.

November is spent preparing for the tree going up the first week of December. Mam starts her Christmas clean, and every inch of the house gets a good going over.

"I like the house to twinkle, especially at Christmas," she tells me, "My mother didn't have two shillings to rub together but she kept the best house on the street. She always did an extra Christmas clean."

We make the Christmas cake, and she starts putting special tinned and packet food on the top shelf of the pantry. She calls it squirrelling. Dad loves Christmas even more than we do. It's him who likes the tree up early.

"Why wait?" he asks, "it lights up the dark days of December a treat."

It's been snowing since the end of October off and on. It's either coming or going all winter and dad says we get more because we live on higher ground. We're used to it being there and it gives us a few extra days off school a year because the bus can't always get through and it's too far to walk. We all go into the woods to sledge on those days. Mam moans and says it takes her ages to get me warmed up and dried out when I come in, but she doesn't mind really. We usually have hot milk and custard cream biscuits by the fire, and I look forward to it all the time I'm sledging. I haven't been this year because Margaret can't so I wouldn't enjoy it, thinking about her sitting in bed.

On 30th November, we take our annual trip after school to the Post Office on the main street to buy my cardboard advent calendar. There's only one kind to choose from and this year it's a painting of a cottage in the snow with a Christmas tree in the garden. It's a nice one, but then they always are.

I ask mam if we can buy an extra one for Margaret as it doesn't cost too much.

"Her mam says it's okay," I tell her.

I don't know why I told a lie but afterwards I think it was only a white lie because Margaret will love it and if her mam says no, I'll sneak it in and hide it. I don't understand what all the fuss is about. I just think it would be lovely for her to have it and to be able to open a window every day.

The next day is a Wednesday and I'm thinking about putting the tree up all day at school. I told Margaret I'd be a bit late. Mam's waiting for me with a pot of tea and a mince pie.

"I bet you haven't managed to get a stroke of work done all day at school, have you?" she laughs, "I know you're excited, but we need to eat before we do anything else. Strength goes in at the mouth."

She says that all the time. She told me once that her mam and dad were so short of money when she was growing up, she can never take food for granted. She says we don't know we're born nowadays as we have everything we want.

It's fine though because I like a little build up to doing the tree.

Last January we bought a white one and some new coloured lights in the sale. We measured it to be sure we could put it on a small table in the window like everyone else. We always need to move the chair and coffee table forward a bit to fit it in. We get a new bauble every year too, but we still hang up the old ones and even some I made when I was small.

"It's not a showhouse, it's not a department store tree, it needs to be a tree filled with memories for a home," she says.

She's right and I'll have one just like it when I get my own house, I think.

When it's finally decorated and lit after about an hour, we turn off the lamp and sit by the fire. I have a sherry with mam in my special glass and just sit staring at it. The house is quiet without the television on but it's not long before we can hear the c'workers chatting on their way home. Mam says even though we can't hear their boots in winter because of the snow, they still make as much racket as a few hundred old washer women. Dad will be home too, any minute but he always hangs back until everyone else is in the house on tree-trimming day.

When it finally goes quiet again, dad knocks on the door, and we get up to meet him. We've got our coats on already, so we just put our wellies on which are waiting on the newspaper. It's the only time we use the front door and when we open it, dad's grinning all over his dirty face at the bottom of the steps.

"My ladies," he says, bowing his head as he helps us down the steps.

We've been so warm by the fire the cold takes a bit of getting used to. Making our way over the road to stand in our usual positions by the woodland we turn and stare at the new coloured lights on the tree in our window. It's always the first to go up in the town by a mile.

"Well, I for one think it's the best yet," dad says, putting his arms around us.

He says that every year, but somehow it is. I'm glad we got a white tree for a change.

After tea, I run around the front of the house to have another look at the tree before I set off down to see Margaret. On the way, I bump into Brian Addlebury and his daughter, Ruth. I think they must be going to Sally Evans's shop.

I don't know what it is about Brian, but he gives me the colly wobbles. It's just a feeling and everybody likes him, so I don't know why. She's nice looking, and always wears posh clothes but you never see her smile. Still, her mam died so you wouldn't really, I suppose.

"Hello," I say, because mam always tells me we should never pass anybody in the street without saying it.

They walk on as though I'm not there. Rude beggars, I think, wait until I tell Margaret. They always talk to me if

I'm with dad because he's above Brian at *Worthies*. I hate people like that.

By the time I've got to Margaret's, I've calmed my temper. It doesn't flare often but when it does, you know about it.

"Go on up, love," Aunt Esther says after I step into their kitchen and place my wellies on the rack.

She looks tired and her hair isn't as tidy as usual. I start to wonder if everything's alright as she doesn't say any more. She generally asks me how mam and dad are, so I start to panic.

"Is Margaret, okay?" I ask her.

"Oh, yes, sorry Dolly, I've just been running around getting us organised for the trip to the Infirmary tomorrow. I wish they could come here but of course they can't bring all the equipment with them."

She laughs a funny peculiar laugh.

I think about the nice teatime I've just had with mam and dad by the tree and feel sorry for them all. I don't mention the advent calendar or trimming up Margaret's room. She's got enough on and somehow, I can't bring myself to ask.

Uncle Robert's sitting reading his paper in the front room. It looks bare and dismal compared to ours at home.

"Alright, love?" he asks, and I tell him I'm fine and ask if he is.

"Can't grumble," he says, looking up from his paper and giving me a smile.

He still looks sad. It makes me sad too and suddenly I wish I was at home.

Now, don't you be so selfish, Dolly Hunter, I think.

Margaret's waiting for me with the telly on. She has a small fireplace in her room and the fires always lit in winter as she feels the cold. I'm glad of it tonight as it looks so welcoming.

"Did you get your tree up?" she asks me when I'm sitting down in the little pink velvet chair by her bed. I look at her for a second or two.

"I don't feel right talking about it this year, Maggie, if I'm honest, it's like I'm rubbing it in. Like I'm showing off."

"Don't be daft, I want you to describe it to me in every detail. I love to come to your house at Christmas time. I wish mam would keep Christmas like your mam. Dad does too, I know he does. I bet they don't even put the tinsel up this year as I'm up here. It's a shame."

So, Margaret does think about Christmas then. I remember now how I can put the smile back on her face.

"I've got something which will cheer you up."

"Oh, how nice, Dolly. What's that then?"

"I've got you an advent calendar like mine so you can have a countdown to Christmas. I'll think of something nice for us to do on Christmas Day even if it's on the quiet. I don't want to get you into bother, so I was going to check with your mam first about the calendar. I was even going to mention about trimming up your room, but I chickened out because she looks done in."

I wish I hadn't said that because Margaret looks guilty and doesn't say anything. I'm mad at myself now.

My cheeks burn and I quickly pick my bag off the floor to rummage about for mam's magazine which I wrapped around the calendar so it wouldn't get squashed. Margaret's eyes start twinkling just like our tree and she opens her mouth in surprise when I hand it to her. I'm even more pleased I got it for her now.

"Oh, Dolly, I've always wanted one of these! I've seen them at your house."

She runs her hand over the cardboard and sticks her thumbnail under the flap of number one. It reveals a candle behind a window, like mine did earlier this morning. She looks like I've given her the world wrapped up with a bow on top.

"What about your mam?" I ask.

She thinks for a minute.

"You can bring it every night and we can open a window together. I can't risk her taking it off me or getting in a mood. I just can't."

So that's what we do, at least for a couple of weeks.

When I'm walking home, I remember I never got around to telling Margaret the story of Brian Addlebury and snotty Ruth ignoring me.

But we had more important things to think about than them two.

Chapter 5

"Well, it can come tomorrow for me," mam says, exactly two Wednesdays later.

I'm all set for school, shovelling down my cornflakes and toast. I was a bit late getting up and already felt behind with myself. I'm not really listening to the tight schedule as she calls it that she had to stick to so she could get organised early. I nod along and pretend I'm listening though.

"Just the hairdressers for my rinse after work today and I'm done."

She smiles and runs her blondish hair through her fingers on each side of her head. It bounces straight back into curls. Dad bought her some heated rollers a couple of years ago and she uses them every morning. Her hair was as straight as a poker before he got them at Sally Evans's for her birthday. All my friends tell me how pretty mam is. If I mention it, she just says a lady should try and make the best of herself.

"You're quiet this morning," she says.

"The bus is due in five minutes," I tell her, "I'm all out of sorts because I hate chasing my tail."

She laughs.

"Chasing your tail; I ask you. Get your things on and be off with you, miss," she says, handing me my coat.

That makes me laugh and she gives me a kiss as I'm putting my arm through.

On the bus, I remember I didn't even have time to open my advent calendar window this morning. It makes me think about Margaret. They told her at the Infirmary she'll have to go more often in the new year. I hope the day improves so then my mood will. I give a big sigh without realising and Christine Cooper stops talking to Diane Harris to ask what's bothering me.

"Oh, I'm alright, just ignore me," I say.

They know what's good for them when I'm in a mood, so they do, and Christine carries on describing the new boots she's going to get for Christmas. I wish boots were all I had to worry about, I think. Everything seems so unimportant when you're worried about somebody who's ill.

Thankfully, it's Christmas dinner day in the school canteen and that puts me in a better mood. It's a bit on the cold side but not bad on the whole. I eat dinner with Christine and Diane as usual, looking forward to the day Margaret gets back to school so we can be a foursome again. Mam says three never agree, but we're doing alright.

It's English then History in the afternoon and I'm not with Christine and Diane in either class so I tell them I'll see them on the bus home.

We've only got about fifteen minutes to go before the end of school when Mr Fleming, our headteacher, knocks loudly and walks into our history class. He looks like he's trying to act normal but he's red in the face and he's definitely not being normal. He's usually as stiff as a board.

"Mr Carr, please can I have a word with you."

Mr Carr immediately looks flustered, as though he thinks he's in trouble.

"Certainly, sir," he answers quick as a flash, dropping his chalk rubber on his desk with a clatter.

We all look at each other and start whispering about what Mr Carr could have done. He's not bad as teachers go, so we can't imagine. I can see Mr Fleming talking to him through the glass door and Mr Carr is nodding with a worried look on his face. I turn round quickly before he sees me but then I notice all the class is doing the same.

He walks to the front of the classroom, and we wait for what seems like ages for him to speak. He clears his throat.

"Mr Fleming has asked if the pupils from Wakeley can make their way to the library. There's nothing to worry about, he just needs to talk to you before you go home," he tells us in his loud voice, "get your things together and head to the library quietly, please."

This is weird, I think as I cram everything in my bag. I can feel Keith Fieldhead, who I sit next to for History, looking at me, but I don't look at him. I just want to get out of the classroom and find out what's going on.

It's always quiet in the library of course, but when I walk in tonight it's creepy. I don't know how many of us live in Wakeley because I've never thought about it, but I know there's enough for a bus load. Mr Fleming's ticking us off his list.

"Find a seat, I'm just waiting for everyone to get here," he says.

I see Christine and Diane but there's no space next to them, so we wave, and I sit next to people I know but not well enough to be friends with. I'm glad because I'm not bothered for talking. The last few finally come in to join us exactly three minutes later. I know it's three minutes because I've been watching the clock the whole time.

"All right, settle down," he starts. His voice is squeaky and me and Christine raise our eyebrows at each other across the room. She looks pale and I wonder if I do too.

"Now everyone's here, I just want to tell you what will be happening when you get off the bus tonight. There's nothing to worry about but when you get to Wakeley, you'll be getting dropped off at the community hall."

He hesitates, and his mouth opens and closes so I wonder what he's about to say. My stomach ties itself in a knot.

"There's been an incident at *Worthington's* this afternoon, so your parents are going to meet you there first and you can have some tea and biscuits while they get things sorted properly." Yet another pause. "That will be nice, won't it?" he asks.

He smiles but he looks scary, and nobody smiles back.

"I know you'll all have lots of questions, but we think it's best for them to be answered when you're back home with your families. I'll be coming with you so don't worry."

"Now if we can all make our way to the pickup point in an orderly fashion," he says, suddenly back to being headmaster again.

He stands up and directs the front table out of the library, herding them all like sheep.

Sitting here waiting to join the queue out of the door, I'm thinking that three times now we've been told not to worry.

But somehow, I feel as worried as I've been feeling about Margaret, even if it is in a different way.

*

I sit and stare at Mr Fleming's bald patch the whole way home on the bus.

Christine is next to me, and Diane is behind next to Brenda. I think they feel sorry for me because of Margaret not being around so they always split up and Brenda will sit next to anyone who'll let her because she's quiet and not very popular. I think about how Margaret's quiet but she's one of the most popular girls in school, so it can't be just that.

Everyone's chattering about what they think might have happened at *Worthies*, but they've run out of ideas now. The bus can't get us home quick enough for my liking. I wonder if mam managed to get her hair done, I think suddenly out of nowhere.

The bus driver doesn't go the usual way into Wakeley. Before we reach the village, he detours up the narrow lane which skirts the village to the east before winding its way up to meet the road up to the neighbouring village of Erdington. It's narrower and tricky in the snow, but it's not too deep just yet.

"Do you think we're going this way, so we don't go past *Worthies*?" Christine whispers.

I hadn't thought of that, so I start to feel a bit sick. It must be. I give her a nod and we sit looking at each other a minute.

The bus stops at the back of the hall and Mr Fleming gets up to talk to us.

"Now, like I said please make your way inside quietly. There's no rush and don't worry if your parents aren't there because some are helping to get things sorted. I'll see you all in there shortly."

He gets off the bus and starts ticking his list for the third time today.

I've got my coat on but I'm still shivering. I stay close to Christine and Diane as we go inside. They've lit the fire at the far end of the room and there's people everywhere, even some that aren't mams and dads. Diane gets pulled away by her mam almost straight away so, I'm glad to still have Christine but then a minute later her mam grabs her too. She's looking over her shoulder at me as she's walking away. It's all very busy and unorganised in here. My eyes are searching all over the room, but I can't find my own mam.

My stomach starts rolling but then I see Aunt Esther rushing around and she must be looking for me as her face lights up when she sees me. She takes me to one side of the room by the window, then she puts her arms around me and holds me tightly. It's strange because she's never done this before. I'm looking at everybody over her shoulder in a daze.

"Aw, Dolly, I'm so glad you're back. Don't worry about your mam she's over at *Worthies* helping out. Mrs Turrell's with our Margaret."

How kind of her to come for me when she will have been at the hospital all day with Margaret.

"What's happened?" I ask.

She stares into my eyes for a minute, so I start to feel hot.

"There's been a fire," she says finally, "they've got it all under control now though, love so don't look so worried."

I'm not really concentrating because while Aunt Esther is talking, I can hear Joyce Pinner's voice behind me saying to someone, "I heard it was some stupid idiot who dropped a ciggie in the wood store next to the finishing room. Most were in the canteen having dinner, but there were some up on the top floor. It took hold quickly."

Oh, the relief. They've got it all under control so everything's going to be alright, Aunt Esther said so. I lean against the wall by the window and put my bag on the floor because I'm suddenly very tired.

"Come on, lass," she says, "hot sweet tea for you and you'll be good as new. Today's a day we'll never forget and that's for sure."

"You're right there, Aunt Esther," I say.

Mrs Worthington's organising the tea and biscuits. She looks odd in her smart clothes and high heels, with her hair up, but she's chatting to everybody as she's pouring their tea. I find a seat as near as I can to the fire and wait for Aunt Esther to come back.

I look around the room as I'm waiting, taking it all in. Shuffling in my seat the hairs on my arms stand up as I notice people whispering and then turning back around when they catch me looking at them. I have that sick feeling again, and I want my mam to come and get me. I want her to come right now. They've got the fire under control, so surely, she should be on her way.

Just as I get up to go over and tell Aunt Esther I'm going to *Worthies*, Ralph, who's sitting with his mam and gran, shouts, "Dolly, your mam's here now," and I see her walk into the hall.

Thank goodness, I think throwing my bag over my shoulder to make my way over to her. I've never felt relief like it.

Then everything seems to go in slow motion like you see on the telly almost straight afterwards. Aunt Esther is walking towards me and so is Mr Fleming. Mam doesn't look like my mam. I just know instantly and without anyone telling me that something bad has happened. I think of dad. I don't know why I didn't think about him before. I feel guilty that I was only thinking about mam for some reason, but Aunt Esther told me it was all under control. She did.

Standing in front of mam she looks at me for a second like she's never seen me before, and then she puts her arms around me. I understand why Aunt Esther did that now.

I can feel mam gently shooing Aunt Esther and Mr Fleming away behind my back. I hold onto her, and I don't want to move but I also don't want to stay in this hall. She knows without me telling her, keeping her arm around me as we walk away. I don't look but I know everyone is looking at us and I fight an urge to run.

Our house seems a long way away. As we cross the road, mam tries to pull my face back under her arm, telling me not to look, but I get a glimpse of *Worthies*. One corner of the building is gone and the stone around is all black. There's a police car and three fire engines outside.

I can see Mrs Turrell watching us going down the path through her nets. When we finally get in, we close the door behind us. Mam pulls my coat off and sits me by the fire, putting more coal on and poking at it to get it going again. She sits down in the chair opposite and puts her head on the back. Her face is like a stone.

"Uncle Robert's just come back from the hospital with me. Mr Worthington picked us up in his car," she tells me.

I nod, but I can't think of anything to say. I know now what's happened. I'm old enough to realise she'd still be at the hospital if …

She's looking at me but not into my eyes, and her face is white as a sheet. She didn't get her hair done.

"I'm so sorry, love," she says, as though it's her fault.

Dragging her arms out of her coat, she drops it to the floor. Poor mam, I think. I want it to be last night when we were all sitting together before I went to bed. Me and mam were writing Christmas cards and dad was laughing at something on the telly. My throat is tight and painful.

I start to babble some words to try and help her feel better.

"We'll be alright, mam," I tell her, "We'll look after each other and we'll be fine, I know we will."

I don't know we will, but I can't think of anything better to say. I keep swallowing to try and hold the tears in. She gives me a little smile that makes a tear fall down my cheek and I wipe it away quickly hoping she didn't notice.

"You've always been too old for your years, Dolly. It must come from being an only child."

I know why I'm an only one, but I wish I wasn't for once. I want to see Margaret but that's selfish. I can't leave mam on her own. I can't help it; my face crumples up and I start to sob. Mam kneels at my feet and rubs my cold hands. I feel bad for crying when she's got enough on. I want to ask about dad, but I don't want to know. It's all so confusing; too confusing.

After a while, she gets up from the floor to go into the kitchen.

"There's nothing more to be done tonight, love, so I'll do us some tea and toast. If we can't eat it, we leave it."

This is the first time she's ever said we can leave food.

We sit in the dark until late. The gate goes from time to time, and I know people will be leaving bunches of flowers in the back yard. There'll be more tomorrow and then there'll be people coming with pies and stews for weeks. That's what always happens when someone dies. That's what we do for others. I try not to think about dad and where he is now. I try to keep my mind blank but nasty little images keep making their way in. I'm swallowing and swallowing because I'm determined not to cry again.

I try not to look at the unlit Christmas tree. It seems dead now and think I won't want to put it up again. I know I'll never be able to enjoy looking at it because it will remind me how I feel tonight.

When the clock strikes ten, mam says it's time for me to go to bed. She hasn't spoken for ages I realise, and I don't want to leave her on her own even though I really want to be on my own.

"Go on up, love, it won't change anything, us sitting down here all night. There's plenty to do tomorrow. I'll be on my way up soon."

I pick up the cups and plates from the coffee table and go into the kitchen. I leave the ashtray because I've lost count of the number of cigarette's she's had but it looks like she's still going. I put the toast in the bin and rinse the plates and cups, so she doesn't have to do it.

Then I go back into the dark room and kiss her cheek. She smiles and holds onto my hand so I can't move. She's rubbing her thumb over my wrist, staring at it and I can only hear the fire crackling. It makes me uncomfortable.

"I asked Aunt Esther the other day if Margaret liked her advent calendar, but she said she didn't know anything about it."

I wasn't expecting that. It's like a slap in the face and I want to pull my arm away and go to bed.

"It's just you and me now, Dolly, so don't you ever lie to me again."

I can't look at her, I'm so ashamed.

"I'm sorry, mam, I won't ever do it again, I promise."

She drops my wrist and I'd like to run upstairs, but I walk.

"I'm glad," is all she says, as I'm at the foot of the stairs.

As I get under the cold sheets with tears streaming down my face, I wonder why she had to say that, tonight of all nights. But now I know grief and loss can make people do all kinds of strange things you can't explain.

When I get up in the morning my advent calendar is in the dresser drawer and the Christmas trees down from its spot in the window and back in its box.

It's down and it never goes back up again.

51

Chapter 6
Dolly Now

They're both stood staring at me in my back yard, like two drowned kittens.

 I'd say rats but they look too pathetic for that. I'd just got done and turned the telly on when there was a knock on the door. I ignored it the first time, but I knew even while I was doing it, they wouldn't give in so easily because they knew I was in.

"Sorry," Ralph says, rain dripping off the end of his nose, "I've run out of ideas now the weather's bad and she asked if we could come and see you."

He nods down at the bairn who's smiling at me from under her red hood. I look at them both for a second, but I know there's no getting out of this one easily and they're a pitiful sight. I sigh under my breath and pull the door back.

They take their shoes off politely and I take their wet coats and hang them at each end of the kitchen radiator. What he thinks I'm supposed to do with her, I don't know.

I nod for them to sit down and join them in my chair by the fire.

"I'll switch this off now I've got company," I say.

"No, don't," the bairn says, "I watch it with grandpa sometimes. I love it."

"That's if Miss Dolly doesn't mind," Ralph says quickly.

Her eyes and mouth grow wide, horrified at speaking out of turn.

"Oh yes, sorry, if you don't mind."

I shake my head, so she shifts herself back on the settee. That's twice she's mentioned her grandpa but no dad. Funny old set-up. She's got a different football shirt on, same team, with a long-sleeved shirt underneath. Her curls are lopsided on the top of her head and the knees of her jeans have two large mud stains. So, she had a go in goal today then, rain or not.

"It's going to be a long winter if you don't get something sorted," I say to Ralph, who's wiping his face with his crumpled white hankie.

He's bitten off more than he can chew. I knew he was too hasty offering to look after her when he's no idea about seven-year-olds or children in general. I'm the same, but I know my limitations.

He runs his fingers through his hair and sniffs.

"I've put a few posters out to see if I can drum up any interest in a five-a-side team for her. Sally Evans is asking around and Harriet says Thorndale Primary have a football team so they can have a few kickabouts."

"You'll have your work cut out finding four kids around here of a similar age."

"They don't have to be a similar age they just need to enjoy playing a game of football."

"I was in a football team at my school in Leeds," the bairn tells me, proudly, "they were all boys, but they let me play."

"How did you find out you liked football?" I ask.

It's a strange sport for a girl if you ask me but I suppose I'm not up with the times.

"My dad and my grandpa support Leeds United so we've always watched their matches together. We have pork pie and tomato sauce while we're watching. Well, they have brown sauce."

I want to ask where they are, but I can't without it sounding nosy, so I keep quiet. I look across at her and Ralph watching the telly and wonder how on earth I got roped into this. I get up to the go into the kitchen.

"I'll do us some tea," I mutter but nobody's listening.

I come back in with a tea tray and biscuits and they both scoot to the front of their seats.

"Oh, thank you very much Mrs Dolly, I love custard creams," she says.

I open my mouth to correct my title but think better of it. I can't be bothered.

"Does your mum like her new job?" I ask.

"Yes, she does thanks. She says Mr Lockwood makes her laugh but she's very busy as there's a lot to do."

He makes everyone laugh, does Bernie, he's the town joke if truth be told and he doesn't earn his keep that's for sure. The bins didn't get collected one week and it was pandemonium. When I asked him about it, he said he'd forgotten to speak to the person in Environmental health at the Council. I ask you, a councillor that doesn't talk to the council. They haven't forgotten again mind.

"Would you take the £8,500?" asks Ralph, fixated on the screen and the gameshow. His check shirt looks like it needs a good iron, but then I suppose he has been playing football. Sometimes when I look at him, I find myself wondering where all the years have gone. He makes me very aware of the passing of time, more so than looking at my own face in the mirror.

"Certainly, I would, anything over £5,000 is being greedy if you ask me. I'd rather have £5,000 in my hand than £250,000 in the bush."

Ralph chuckles.

"Well, there'd not be much of a show then, Dolly if everybody felt like you. It's called taking a risk."

He pulls a face and rolls his eyes, so the bairn starts laughing. I look at the pair of them in turn. They're a right couple of partners in crime, if ever there was one. I can't help it. My mouth is twitching as I turn to look into the fire.

I pour the tea and we sit and watch the telly for a while in silence, with only the background noise of biscuits being crunched and the fire. It's still going strong and I'm glad because the rain looks like it's turning to snow. I only like to go out for coal once a day if I can help it.

Placing my empty teacup on the tray I look up to see they're both snoozing. Ralph's heads fallen to one side on the chairback, and Lydia's curled up with her feet under her. I look at her tiny face, glowing from the heat of the fire and her small mouth slightly open. She's bonny mind, I think, dainty featured.

Ralph wakes himself up with a snore, apologising immediately, still half asleep.

"Don't worry," I tell him absentmindedly, still looking at the bairn's face on the arm of my settee.

I must admit, I've had worse afternoons.

*

At four o'clock Ralph says he needs to get the bairn back home. We've had another cup of tea and discussed the fact Lydia likes to be in goal because Mr Pritchard said she has a talent for goal keeping and she finds herself getting all excited when the ball gets nearer. If they can drum up enough interest, they're going to use the old primary school playing field because her mum said Mr Lockwood says it's ok, but he might have to look into insurance or something.

Insurance indeed, for ten kids to kick a ball around for an hour a week. I ask you. If any kid broke their leg playing football when I was growing up, their mothers just thought they were unlucky at best or silly sods at worst. They wouldn't have thought about suing the council, I know that much.

"I'll walk with you," I tell him, "I need to do the vicar's shopping, so I might as well do it before the snow settles."

"I forgot to tell you, Mrs Dolly," the bairn pipes up as we get to their gate, "mum said she'd love it if you'd come for afternoon tea next Saturday now that we've got settled in. Would you be able to come after you've done your jobs in church?"

I'm agitated, unprepared for the question. The last time I was in that house, Margaret was there, and I don't know if I can face going in now. I never thought I'd need to.

"I think I might be a bit tired after church," I tell her quickly, "but thank your mum for the kind offer and maybe she'll call for a cup of tea one day when she's free."

I watch the fall of her face. I'd no idea it would mean so much to her and I somehow feel terrible for being the culprit of her forlorn expression. Ralph glances my way.

"You're only sitting and supping tea, Dolly. I'm sure it would make their day if you went."

I'm tetchy with him for pushing me, but I know he's right. I look down at the bairn's face tilted upwards, waiting expectantly for my answer.

"Tell your mum I would be happy to come. I'll get here for four o'clock if I don't hear otherwise."

"That's just brilliant," she says grinning, "me and mum can do some baking on Saturday morning."

I smile down at her.

"Wash your hands first, mind," I tell her.

"I will," she shouts on her way up the path, and Ralph smirks and shakes his head before he follows behind.

I turn right now to Sally Evans's. The peeling *Bile Beans* sign she was paid a fortune for displaying on the side of the shop years ago has snowflakes clinging half-way up it already. She's taken everything she normally displays outside inside.

Sally is on her own in the shop, writing in her old leather-bound ledger that's never far away. She told me once she should move onto technology, but she'd be all at sixes and sevens if she did. She knows exactly what's come in and what's gone out with stock and with money using her tried and tested system. It sounds fair enough to me.

"Hello there, Dolly, I've got your staples put by in the back, so you just need the extras," she says, heading off to get them.

I thank her and park my trolley in front of the wood-panelled counter. I hate using the trolly because it makes me feel like an old woman but it's better if I shop for the week for the vicar and get my own groceries in between.

"Have you seen much of the newcomers over the last few weeks?" she asks.

Hardly surprisingly, they're all everybody talks about now. It's a long time since we had new faces in Wakeley.

"Here and there," I say, "I've just had Ralph and the bairn round at mine this afternoon."

She looks surprised, as well she might. I'm surprised.

"I must say they're a breath of fresh air don't you think? So sweet and polite. Endearing, my mother would have called them."

"Yes, they seem alright enough," I answer, "but then we've only known them two minutes."

I pick some new peas up and put them down, deciding on the cheaper brand. Peas are peas.

"I hope they can get a team going. I'd go watch them and I know my Ted would. Ralph would be like a pig in muck as head coach. Can you imagine?"

She laughs at the thought. She laughs a lot does, Sally. She's kindly by nature and it makes her popular which is always handy when you're a shopkeeper. She's older than me and I'm aware she looks younger, but then she likes a fair bit of preening. Her dark hair is from a bottle, and she goes to the hairdressers in Thorndale once a week to have it set.

Knocking on they might be, but her and Ted don't show any sign of wanting to retire. I'm pleased about that. I don't know what we'd do without this shop, I think more and more lately. I push myself to get as much as I can manage without going mad and there's still enough of us to keep it going at my last count … just about.

I grab the other extras on my list and head back to the counter to pay from my special purse I keep for the vicar's money.

"See you tomorrow, Dolly," Sally shouts, on my way out, "let me know if you find anything else out."

I won't, I think but I lift my arm and wave to her without turning round.

At the vicarage I let myself in with my key then put the groceries away before I head to the study to see the vicar. I like to spread the work out, so I don't have cleaning to do today, and he couldn't care less when I do it, just so long as it gets done.

It's a pleasure to clean this beautiful house. I actually enjoy it as much as doing my own and I've done it so long, it feels like mine anyway. I used to come with mam when she did the job before me and help her with little tasks like emptying bins, and such.

The vicar's often out so I have a cup of tea in the kitchen before I leave and admire the gleam of the black and white floor tiles and the warm glow of the polished wood table. I always light the fires as my last job so it's a nice bit of peace and quiet listening to the crackle in the black-leaded range for a while.

I head down the passageway to the study and knock on the door.

"Come in, Dolly," he shouts, "I thought you might come tonight on account of the snow."

"Good afternoon, vicar," I greet him and start bustling about tidying newspapers and such. I do it on autopilot even if it's not a cleaning day because I like to see it looking just so.

"I'm glad I'm in to catch you because I've been meaning to have a word."

"Really," I say, passively though I'm immediately on edge.

He nods and takes his glasses off. Grey or not, like Ralph he's still got a full head of hair. There must be something in the water round here. The only difference is Ralph's hair is white grey. Everybody compliments him on it when he bothers to comb it properly.

"Two things: One, I'm going to up your wages. It's long overdue and remiss on my part so I apologise."

"No need for that," I say, "it's a pleasure and an honour."

I wonder then if he pays me or the church but that's none of my business. Well, that was painless enough, I think, so what's next? He smiles at me, and I wait for him to continue.

"The other thing is that the new young lady, Harriet Scott has asked if she can try and form a choir for a Christmas concert. I thought this was a delightful idea and I always welcome thoughts on how to bring people together as you know, Dolly."

I nod but wonder what this has to do with me. I draw the curtains, shutting out the snow that's coming down harder now.

"I was wondering if you'd consider doing some refreshments for them if she manages to encourage enough interest. I know you thoughtfully volunteer to organise the church, but you could do less on Saturdays in order to balance your time, if this would help."

Time—I'm not bothered about the time, I think, that's not a problem. I'm bothered about being roped into yet another aspect of this stranger's life I didn't sign up to. I struggle to disguise my annoyance but manage to succeed, I hope. It's not the vicar's fault, he's just the messenger. Anyway, he's in charge in my book so I'm backed in a corner yet again.

"I don't see a problem," I lie, "perhaps you could keep me updated as to when it might start."

I want to say if or when it might start. Much like the football, I doubt she'll have enough takers thankfully.

"I will indeed, and I thank you for your support as always, Dolly."

I incline my head and bid him farewell, fighting the urge to slam a door on my way out.

Locking up I think about the changes which are being brought about by two, well one, busybody in such a short period of time. She's causing upset and it seems I'm just supposed to go along with it.

The wind's getting up and it's biting my face as I head down the road towards home in the snow. Everybody's tucked up inside and I notice the lights are off at Sally's shop.

I'm glad when I get back on the other side of my own door where I'm back to the comfort and security of my own world again. Where I'm the one in control.

I look around the room, an uneasy thought appearing from nowhere.

It feels different. It's not quite the sanctuary it once was for some reason and as I head to the kitchen to put the kettle on, I'm wishing Saturday and my trip down the road for afternoon tea had been and gone already.

Chapter 7
Dolly Then

"I still don't know why you had to marry him," I say.

He's down at the pub like every night, and we're washing up in the kitchen after tea; second sitting. Her ladyship's gone up to bed, so we have to whisper as her room is above us. Well, I should say our room now.

"For heaven's sake, Dolly," mam hisses, "we've been through all this time and time again. I know it's different now it's not just you and me but he's not nearly as bad as you like to make out."

Turning away she piles the dried plates in the top cupboard over the fridge. She does right, not looking at me; we both know she's having herself on. I stare out into the back yard as I finish off the washing up and try to settle myself down. I'm like a stuck record, but I have to get it off my chest or I'll go barmy.

"Look, I know it's been hard for you with your dad and Margaret gone but just because Ruth keeps herself to herself doesn't make her evil, as you like to make out. Ralph seems to see something we don't, or they wouldn't be getting married."

Ralph's taken in by anybody, I think. Ruth wanted him, so she was going to have him, no mistake. She's used to getting everything she wants; her father sees to that.

"The thing that sets my teeth on edge the most is how fake he is outside the house. Everybody thinks the sun shines out of his backside, you know they do. That riles me up more than anything else."

I nearly say arse because I'm so worked up, but I manage to stop myself. Mam was one of those who thought he was something different than he turned out to be, but he worked his charm on her for long enough until he got his feet under the table. I saw through him … and her. You can't ignore a gut feeling. You shouldn't ignore it if you've any sense.

"You'll understand when you're older, Dolly, not everything's black and white. I was scared for both of us, for our futures. Mr Worthington saw us alright, but he wouldn't be able to keep us going forever. Nor should he.

I know what she's thinking. She's thinking dad was to blame for what happened. He was the one smoking in the toilet and many more could have been made husbandless and fatherless. She's thinking it's not easy to look people in the eye anymore because we're so ashamed.

"No, he's been more than fair with us considering has Mr Worthington, but then he always was a gentleman."

I sigh and pull the plug out of the sink, reaching for a towel.

"All I'm saying is he's devious is Brian, which is the worst kind of mental torture in my book. Like, he knows how you feel about food and feeding your family, yet he eats with her and then we have to eat when he's gone out and she's gone upstairs, or off with Ralph. That's two lots of teas to cook every night to start with. Then there's the fact he doesn't like you to dye your hair blonde, so he won't give you the money. You used to love faffing about with your hair. He's controlling, that's what he is. He likes to make sure you know he's in charge and you should be grateful for him keeping us. I can't wait to start in the office at *Lumley's*. No more Cinderella then, we can manage without his money if you'll give him the boot. I just wish people knew the real Brian Addlebury."

I don't mention I hear her quietly crying in the toilet most nights after he's got back from the pub. She thinks I'm asleep, but I can't settle until long after mam has gone back to bed. She would only tell me it's none of my business.

Except I think it is really because she is *my* mother.

"Controlling, indeed. I don't know where you hear these phrases. Him and Ruth have had hard times too. He raised her for three years on his own after Doreen died and it's not easy being a mother and a father to a teenager. I should know."

Yes, she should. Taking a deep breath, I decide I'm just talking to myself. I give in. I may as well change the subject.

"How long have we got before the wedding of the year?"

Mam smiles and rolls her eyes. It's a rhetorical question because I know full well.

Ten and a half months and counting, is how long. Ten and a half months of sharing a room with her when she barely looks the side I'm on. That's another kind of controlling, but I'll not let her get the better of me. I hope Ralph knows what he's doing, is all I can say. She came home with an engagement ring which belonged to Ralph's other gran a while ago, telling her dad he got down on one knee when they were having a picnic in the woods. She's different around Ralph. He's going places and this will suit her mercenary ways.

I decide to think happier thoughts to try and snap out of my mood.

"I've had another letter from Margaret," I tell mam as we make our way into the front room to our chairs by the fire.

It's not roaring up the back of the chimney any longer but it's there. I'm so grateful for these couple of hours of normality. I think I'd do something drastic without them.

"What's going on with them," she asks, all ears, keen to be brought up to date.

We both miss them, but it was the right thing for Margaret to move nearer the Infirmary. The journey was just too hard for everyone involved in the end. The consultant at the hospital used his contacts to set her dad up in a job at a foundry in Leeds and they've rented a lovely house by the sound of it. Other than dad's funeral, it was the hardest thing I've ever done, waving them off that Saturday. I went back inside and sobbed all afternoon in my room. Mam had started seeing Brian by then and I could tell which way they were heading. I was unbelievably lonely and every time I thought of Ruth being in my life, I felt sick. Me and Margaret write to each other every few weeks though and I can't wait to open her letters. She has a notepad with yellow roses on and when I open the envelope there's a pleasant scent. I plan to take a trip to see them all one day, especially now Margaret's doing so well after her operation last year.

"Well, can you believe it?" I ask mam now, "Margaret's fallen for someone. He works with her dad, and they've been going out for six weeks already. His name's Ronnie, he's twenty-three and a bit of a joker but he seems keen, Margaret says, and he makes her laugh. Her mam and dad like him too, I think that's why Uncle Robert introduced them. Margaret says she'll send a picture before too long if they keep going out."

I stare into the fire remembering her lovely smile and shiny dark hair I envied so much. Ronnie had better look after her, I think because we all know he's lucky to have her. There was a time when I secretly didn't think Margaret would make it, never mind start courting. I couldn't be happier for her.

"How's Aunt Esther these days?" mam asks, lighting a cigarette.

"She likes it in Leeds and loves the big house they live in, Margaret said. She keeps herself to herself, but then she always did here so nothing has changed there. Uncle Robert and Margaret are her life, we always said that didn't we?"

"We did. It's not always good for you to put all your eggs in one basket. I was always glad to go to work and have a bit of a life of my own out of the house. I wish Brian would let me go back to *Lumley's* now, but he says he doesn't want any wife of his to work."

"That's not controlling of him, is it?" I say and manage to fake a twinkle in my eye because I don't want to dampen the mood.

Smiling my way, she shakes her head.

"You know, I sometimes long to go back in time, Dolly, when everything seemed so nice and simple and straightforward. If only we'd known it at the time," she says.

I watch her smoking her cigarette, staring into the fire. She looks so sad and wistful, not in the room with me now. I swallow hard. I want to say it could be simple and straightforward again if we worked it out between us. That we could get rid of them both and go back to how life was on our own. That she didn't need to cry in the bathroom every night.

I thought her head was buried deep in the sand then and I'd never be able to make her see sense whatever I said.

I should have had more faith in my mam, I really should.

Chapter 8

I'm looking at myself in the full-length mirror wearing the custom-made turquoise long dress, edged with tiny white daisies at the neckline and the waist. I'm looking at myself wearing a stupid white Juliette cap which squashes the top of my hair and all the while I'm wondering why I've agreed to go along with this fiasco. I hold the white carnation posy between my hands, but it doesn't make me look or feel any better. I know she only wants me to be a bridesmaid because it would look odd otherwise. I should have said no when she asked me, but mam was standing at the back of Ruth with a fixed smile on her face, her eyes almost pleading with me to just play nice.

So, I have. For mam.

I haven't seen the bride-to-be all morning. She's taken over mam's room and we've been getting ready in mine, well mine again after tonight, thank goodness. It's not the same bedroom I used to have. It's full of Ruth's lotions and potions on the windowsill and dressing table and we had to get bunk beds due to it being a small room. Mam and dad took part of it for a bathroom before I was born. Ruth's on the top bunk, and when I watch her bare feet coming down the stepladder on a morning, I slide under the covers thinking I don't want to get up and face the day ahead. Tomorrow just can't come quick enough.

This morning, me and mam have spent ages doing each other's make-up. She looks lovely in her lilac two-piece and cream silky blouse. He graced her with an allowance, for appearances sake of course because appearances will always be everything to him. He was promoted at *Worthies* a couple of months back, but I doubt mam saw any extra money.

Her hair's a bit of a lighter shade; she must have done it herself from a box of dye. She's wearing a cream hat with lilac flowers, and she looks like my beautiful mam for the first time in I don't know how long.

He got himself ready early so he could get out of the way. He's reading the paper downstairs in his suit trousers, his jacket draped over the chair back, ready to be put on at the last minute. I saw it when I went down to get some hair pins out of the dresser and he didn't even look up from his paper. I wasn't bothered because that suits me just fine.

"You look a Bobby Dazzler, Dolly," mam says, and I smile even though it makes my heart tighten.

Dad used to say that.

"So, do you, mam," I say, "is your hair a bit blonder? I like it."

Her face drops, and she immediately puts her hand to the curls falling over her shoulder.

"Is it so noticeable? I only went one shade up."

I should have kept my big trap shut. Now I've made her panic when we were having such a pleasant moment together alone.

"You wouldn't notice unless you were looking closely, don't worry. Anyway, he won't want a fuss today on his beloved daughter's special day, I know that much."

She smiles, placated enough and my stomach settles down a bit.

"I'll just go see how she's getting on," she says.

I hear her knock on the door, and she goes in after being authorised to enter her own bedroom.

Stop it Dolly, I think, today's the day you get that girl out of your life, and she becomes someone else's problem.

I saw Ralph last night and asked him if he was ready for the ball and chain also known as Ruth. It was a straightforward enough comment like most would make. He looked nervous as heck, but he laughed, obviously thinking I was joking. I wanted to set him straight, but mam would be mad at me, and it would only look like I'm jealous and peevish about her. Nobody would believe me anyway so there's no point in telling all the town how miserable we both are.

I step onto the landing and Ruth comes out of the room, mam fiddling with the train of her dress behind her. I think for a minute about it being sad that her mam isn't here but the snotty look on her face soon sees the sadness off. Snotty Ruth, I think. Snotty, snotty Ruth. Ralph needs his head testing.

"Well, Ruth makes a beautiful bride, doesn't she, Dolly?"

"Beeeautiful," I say, for mam's benefit.

Ruth smooths down the front of her dress and chooses to ignore my sarcasm. She probably wasn't even listening. She won't say thank you, she won't say, and you look nice too, like a normal person would but then there's no love lost between us. I gave up trying a long time ago.

Did I really try? I think back to when mam and Brian were going out in the early days. Yes, I did I remind myself, I tried for mam's sake. I even asked her if she missed her mam which might have been a bit too far, but I'd lost my dad, so in theory we had common ground.

"I don't want to talk about it," she told me, "There's no point living in the past."

Her tone of voice told me in no uncertain terms we had no chance of a relationship. She scares me a bit if I'm honest. Brian does too, though I talk a good game to mam when he's out.

I'm Ruth's one and only bridesmaid which says it all. Christine had six at her wedding, including me, because Christine has at least six friends and would have had more bridesmaids if she didn't have to set a limit.

"Dad!" Ruth shouts from the top of the stairs.

I look over the banister and see his head appear around the door. His face lights up for once.

"You look stunning, Ruth," he says, and I see her face smiling from my side view. I have to admit she does. Her hairs up in a soft bun and her veil is draping over one shoulder. It looks like the perfect father-daughter moment, and my throat knots as I think of my dad. I see tears in mam's eyes too as I look over at her. I wish she could be happy again; she deserves it more than anyone. It would make me happy, and I wouldn't ask for another thing ever again in my life, I vow.

We open the door to everyone who's not invited to the wedding waiting patiently to see the bride. They're clamouring outside the gate to get a good look. We love a wedding in Wakeley. Even I love a wedding as a rule, well, after the ceremony when Ralph sneaks me a couple of gins over to put in my tonic water when nobody's looking. He won't be doing that today more's the pity, or ever again now he's getting shackled to her ladyship.

If nothing else, the weather's dry. Dry but dull even though it's summer and it's been sunny for a week. The sun hasn't put in an appearance yet and it makes me think of the saying, "happy the bride the sun shines on". I wish I wanted her to be happy, life wouldn't wear me out so much if I wasn't chewed up with resentment all the time.

The town cheers as she sets off walking down the path, with me trailing behind. Mam picks her dress up and hands me a corner. She looks at me with raised eyebrows and pursed lips, so I take it begrudgingly. Ruth's smiling away at everyone and even throws a sickly one over her shoulder at me and mam. I wish they could all see what I see behind that fake smile, but they think of her as poor motherless Ruth. Oh, for goodness' sake, behave yourself Dolly, I think. Let's just get today over and done with.

As she takes her dad's arm, they smile at each other and lead the procession towards church.

"You look lovely, Dolly," Mrs Turrell says as I close the gate with my free hand.

I'm surprised to be thrown a compliment when I'm not the bride, but I smile and thank her.

The two-minute walk finds us flanked by well-wishers and people passing plastic horseshoes which I have to juggle with my flaming posy and her ladyship's dress. I look at the lace detail and buttons on the back of it as we walk. It pains me to think it, but I'd love a wedding dress like hers one day. If anyone suggests borrowing it though, I'll swing for them I really will.

On the path to the church, I see Sally Evans hopping about, looking all agitated. I think she's overexcited until she suddenly lunges forward and sidles Ruth and her dad to one side. We stop in our tracks when I hear Sally asking them to wait there a moment if they don't mind. I see Brian slide an arm protectively around Ruth's waist as they stand there. Sally walks over to us and I'm bewildered by what's going on. The seriousness of Sally's face makes me start to worry. I realise I've never seen her looking serious before.

"What's going on, Sal?" mam asks, clutching her handbag and putting her other arm through mine.

Sally takes a deep breath and looks like she's struggling with how to string her words together for once.

"Well, how to put it. It's Ralph, we erm, we can't find him. We've been up and down dale for the last half hour."

Can't find him, I repeat in my mind. What a strange thing to say.

Mam looks at Sally then asks a silly question, "Have you checked everywhere you can think of?"

Sally sighs, lowering her head.

"We really have, Joan, everywhere but we kept thinking he'd turn up any minute with some nowt of an explanation. Nothing like this has ever happened before, as you know so we just kept acting like it wasn't happening, so to speak. His gran came to talk to us only a couple of minutes ago or we wouldn't have let you all leave the house."

She pauses then opens her mouth and closes it. There's obviously more to it. We're both looking at her, waiting for more information.

"She thinks he's done a runner."

My own mouth drops. A runner? Ralph? No way, I think, he doesn't have it in him. He's a soft lad is Ralph.

"You need to get her home, Joan, there's no way this wedding's happening today," Sally says, under her breath.

Me and mam stare at each other for a second trying to take it all in. Mam glances over at Brian and Ruth and her face looks like she's scared to go over and tell them. It's not her fault and I'm suddenly annoyed on her behalf. I grab mam's hand and I stride in their direction while mam scurries behind. Brian bristles as we approach, standing taller like he's ready for battle already, while Ruth looks pensive.

"They can't find Ralph," mam whispers to them both, "I'm sorry to tell you his gran thinks he might have," she pauses, "run away."

I watch their faces change before my eyes from confusion to disbelief. I can see each thought happening one by one.

Ruth's face suddenly contorts and reddens like she's having a funny turn. I don't have time to think as she takes me unawares by slapping her bouquet to my chest then grabbing a hunk of my hair in her hands. There are posies and horseshoes flying everywhere, and my hat falls to the ground. I stumble sideways, desperately trying to hold onto my hair at the roots to take the terrible pain away.

She's screaming, "You! You're glad! I can see it all over your face, you're glad to see this happen to me."

I see some spit flying towards me and Mam bats her hand away, while at the same time pushing me behind her back. My scalp's still throbbing.

"Hold on a minute, miss," mam shouts, I've never heard her shout before, "don't take your failings out on our Dolly. Ralph's probably pictured the rest of his life with you spread out before him and run for the hills like any man with any sense!"

I'm so shocked at her outburst I can feel my jaw hanging. I'm shocked but glad all in one. Somebody hands me my hat and I thank them without looking their way as I can't take my eyes off my mother.

I eventually turn my head to see Brian and Ruth are looking at us as if they might kill us. I forget where I am for second but then hear the mutterings going on around us. This wasn't the show everyone turned up for this afternoon.

"Alright, that's enough, get in the house now," Brian says, in a low, threatening voice, looking between all of us. His eyes settle on mam.

I watch her back stretch upwards as far as it will go, until she's towering over the little weasel.

"That's the last time you tell me what to do, Brian Addlebury, get in the bloody house yourself."

The colour rushes up from his neck to his cheeks, and his Adam's apple is Bobbing up and down. He's fast losing control. A cloud passes across his eyes as he raises his clenched fist ever so slightly but thinks better of it when he remembers the crowd around us. The gesture's enough to ignite gasps from our on-lookers though. It's enough to show his true colours, blazing away for all the town to see.

He realises the magnitude of what he's done too late; hitting a woman is down there with the lowest. I imagine the hundreds of men lining up to show you the error of your ways if you tried it.

His pride then taking hold of him, he grabs Ruth's arm, pulling her behind while she trots in her heels trying to keep up. I expect mam to have us bid a hasty retreat somewhere, but she tucks me under her arm, and we join the back of the line of two making their way to our house. Everyone parts the way, and the muttering gets louder.

"Will you be alright, Joan?" Sally Evans asks.

We'll be fine thanks, Sal," mam shouts over her shoulder.

I really hope we will be fine; I really hope she knows what she's doing, I think.

We're walking straight back into the lion's den … and I don't think this particular pair of lions could be any more rattled than they are at this moment.

Chapter 9

We close the door to the sound of the crowd. It will be a while before it disbands, there's plenty to dissect and discuss in stage whispers as dad used to call them. For two pins, I could be sick.

Ruth sits on the settee with her head in her hands, her perfect hair now coming undone. Brian drops his stiff collar onto the coffee table and stays standing. He starts taking his jacket off slowly and it makes him appear intimidating. Mam doesn't look concerned by it though as she ushers me to the chair by the fire and sits opposite.

He paces up and down in front of the settee, and I hear Ruth sniffling quietly. Still staring at the pathetic sight of his daughter he addresses me and mam.

"I hope you're pleased with yourselves, both of you," he says.

What have I done I think aside from getting almost scalped by his nasty piece of work daughter?

"We'll never get over this," he goes on, "we'll never get over the humiliation all round."

His voice is quiet and eerily steady as he stands watching over Ruth who's sitting back in her seat now with panda eyes, staring at the coffee table. I know by "all round" he's referring to his daughter being jilted and him almost giving his wife a right hook in public.

I look across at mam. She's lighting a cigarette, her hands shaking ever so slightly.

"No, you're right, you won't," she says, exhaling smoke.

My eyes go on stalks as I pull my head back like I've just witnessed a man falling off a roof. Oh my, I wasn't expecting that little remark. Brian and Ruth both turn their heads sharply in her direction, no doubt thinking the worm has flipped, never mind turned.

Brian looks like she's slapped his face. He quickly pulls himself together before taking a step towards her.

"You're very full of yourself all of a sudden," he says.

I sit forward, ready to pounce but my mother doesn't need me by the look of her. She straightens her back to sit tall in her chair, staring straight into his eyes.

"If you take a step nearer, you'll be sorry," she says, calmly, though I strongly suspect this isn't how she's feeling.

I wonder if he'll be thinking the same, that she's all bluff and bravado but he must have seen something to bother him. After a couple of seconds, he sits himself down on the other end of the settee. Locking his hands between his spread legs, his elbows on his knees, he drops his head and sighs. He sits still for a minute, thinking, planning, I imagine. I can still hear voices in the street.

"There's nothing else for it. We're going to have to leave, whether we like it or not, there's no other option. We'll have to go tonight, I'm finished in Wakeley. We'll have to stay at my mother's house for the time being until we get sorted. I'll never be able to look anybody in the eye again and neither will she," he says, nodding in Ruth's direction.

She looks a shadow of her former snotty self, but I realise I'm not glad she's been taken down a peg or two and by Ralph of all people. All I can think about is leaving Wakeley.

Mam stares at Brian for a minute, deep in thought.

"Well, I know all about that feeling of shame but for very different reasons, but me and Dolly aren't going anywhere," she says, "we're not leaving our home and certainly not with you."

Her eyes flash, and I wonder yet again what was happening behind closed doors when he got home from the pub all those nights. Ruth must have heard mam crying too if I did.

"You and Ruth are leaving Wakeley, yes, but we're staying put, in the home I lived in with my husband and Dolly lived in with her father."

I'm not sure if I know what that means, but I like the sound of it. However, I think she may be confirming this little plan to herself as much as him, so I mustn't get my hopes up.

Brian looks at my mother like she's grown another head.

"And why would we do that? Like it or not, I'm your husband, we're a family, a poor excuse for one perhaps, but in a family, if one goes, we all go."

She smiles a peculiar smile and I'm wondering again how she can be so defiant so suddenly. This isn't my mam who left the house only half an hour ago.

She takes her hat off slowly and puts it on the coffee table next to the collar. Sitting back in her chair, she crosses her long legs.

"You're a fine one to talk about family" she says, "you of all people."

She looks between Brian and Ruth and shakes her head. They don't know what she means. We all don't.

"I've been biding my time, but now it appears my hand has been forced sooner than expected due to… unforeseen circumstances."

She crosses her hands over her bent knee. Now she even looks confident.

Brian and Ruth are both looking warily at her, wondering what her next words will have in store for them.

"I had an interesting chat the other week with Mrs Turrell," she says.

He shrugs his shoulders, clearly as bewildered as ever.

"What's she got to do with owt? I've never even spoken to her."

A low laugh escapes her, but it doesn't make me feel any better.

"That doesn't surprise me Brian, and it speaks volumes in itself. Why would you? She doesn't have any worth for you. Well, Mrs Turrell pulled me to one side on my way home from the shop a few weeks ago. Apparently, she's heard me crying many a night through the wall as her bedroom is just on the other side of our bathroom. She said it wasn't for her to interfere, but she couldn't take it any longer. I thought I was being quiet about it but obviously not. Anyway, she was happy to provide me with some useful ammunition to tuck away in my pocket for future use."

Ruth's licking her lips, all agitated and he sits up, moving to the edge of his seat.

"She's got nothing on me," he says.

That funny laugh appears again.

"Oh dear, but she has, Brian and she was very happy to share it with me. It seems, you're not a poor lonely widower as you've told everybody these last few years. Doreen didn't go see her mother and then tragically get run over while she was there. No, that's a right cock and bull tale. Mrs Turrell being very vigilant heard a noise one night and as usual, got out of bed to check what it was."

Mam pauses to look at them both on the settee.

"She told me she saw Doreen walking down the road in the dead of night with her bags and get in a taxi. Doreen had to walk a long way to be sure she wasn't seen by anyone who might raise the alarm. Mrs Turrell needed to make her way downstairs and out the front door to make sure she got a proper look. But it was well worth the effort for her. So, your wife ran away in the middle of the night. Imagine Brian; the shame of it."

Ruth looks as floored as I do. She obviously didn't have a clue about her father's lies.

Brian shoots a dagger at mam then quickly turns to his daughter, almost begging, "They're lying, love, they're nasty that's what they are. Why would I do such a thing? I loved your mam. You know I did."

Ruth stares at him for the longest time, as though deciding if he could do such a thing, if he could tell such a shocking lie. He reaches over and tries to put his hand on top of hers, but she knocks it away.

"Get your hands off me," Ruth hisses.

She believes mam, I know she does. It must be like a pain knowing your own mother left you behind when she could have taken you with her.

I can see the cogs turning behind his eyes, planning his next move carefully.

"We can still leave tonight and put all this behind us," he pleads, "you'll never survive on your own, Joan. You tried it once, remember, you didn't like it."

"Ay, you're right but that was then. I thought Dolly and I would have a better future with you but look how that thought blew up in my face."

His change of tac isn't coming off, he knows he's losing. He runs his hand down his face and rubs the side of his neck, his cheeks all puce.

"That woman can't prove anything. It's only her word against mine," he says.

"No, she can't but I think after today everybody will believe her, don't you? Not to mention, I wouldn't want to risk a police investigation for bigamy if I was you. I'd get out quietly while you can, for your own sake, and Ruth's."

I watch a black mascara tear drop down Ruth's cheek onto her dress. It leaves a small stain that grows bigger on the white lace.

"Your time is up around here, Brian Addlebury, the town will never forgive you for the lie, the fake funeral we went to, all the sincere sympathy that was offered, was still being offered, after all these years. You should be ashamed of yourself. As for money, we'll manage. Not that I have to explain owt to you but Dolly's earning more than you are at *Lumley's* and I've spoken to the vicar about the cleaning vacancy and its mine if I want it. Anyway, you can't put a price on happiness and me and Dolly were very happy before you two knocked us both sideways."

As I smile across at my mother, she doesn't notice because her eyes are fixed firmly on Brian.

"If we go, there's no other bloke available in town," he says in desperation, "you'll be on your own for a very long time, if not forever."

"That thought doesn't bother me in the slightest," mam says, putting out her cigarette, "I wouldn't have another fella if he was coughing up diamonds."

I look over at the powerful woman sitting opposite me; she's almost a stranger. I thought she was weak, and she'd put up with anything for us as long as he paid the rent and the bills. I'm disappointed in myself, never mind Brian. I should have known better.

He's beaten, I can see it written all over his ashen face.

Mam nods her head towards the kitchen, and I follow her in. She puts the kettle on as I sit stunned at the kitchen table, watching her make the tea. It's a long time before we speak, even after she sits down. I hear Brian and Ruth going upstairs so I feel ready to talk.

"I'm proud of you, mam," I whisper, breaking the silence.

She puts her hand on mine, and I cover it with my own.

"It was Ruth going for you which made me see red as much as anything else. An instinct kicks in. There's nothing a mother wouldn't do to protect her child. You don't even think about it."

I want to cry with shock but mainly relief, yet I know we're not out of the woods until they're out of the house. Until they're both out of our lives.

We sit at the table until dark drinking tea while we listen to them getting their things together upstairs. After it goes quiet, I start to wonder about Ralph. Where has he gone? Will he be back? Will he be hunted down by Brian and made to pay? I sigh, thinking whatever happens to Ralph, he's well out of it for now. I wish he'd stayed to face the music but then again, he's only a young lad, not much older than me.

I'm drawing the curtains in the kitchen when I hear them coming downstairs. My stomach flips and I follow mam into the front room. Surely, he won't leave quietly like she hopes. He's lost face too much for that.

I watch him getting his money out of the tin in the dresser drawer. I've seen Ruth dib into it a few times but me and mam never would, even though she'd every right.

Ruth's standing with a suitcase in her hand keen to get out and phone for a taxi from the phone box no doubt. She's wearing her jeans with her coat buttoned up, looking pale and strained, so different to last time she left the house. We knew they were hanging about upstairs until it got dark on purpose.

Brian looks over at us as he's stuffing notes into his inner jacket pocket. His wet hair is scraped back from his face so I can see every expression clearly. My legs feel like they might give way, so I hold onto the back of the settee.

"You think you're quite a team, don't you? You think you're so clever and so cute. You'll not look so cocky when you've had a couple of years of scraping by."

"Just go Brian," mam says, "we don't want anything from you, we just want our quiet life back."

His face twists so I find myself running around to the front of mam to get in between them both. He pushes me out of the way and stabs a finger in her face.

"No, but you were happy to take my money when it suited you, the right honourable Mrs Hunter, weren't you," he hisses.

Oh dad, I wish I could close my eyes and you'd come charging through the door to see him off. I'm terrified.

Taking a step backwards, mam stares at Brian in silence, knowing when to keep her mouth shut. He drops his hand and blows out, defeated, looking small again.

"I'll be in touch about the rest of our stuff," he tells her, taking hold of Ruth's arm to guide her out.

She shrugs him off and we step out of the way so they can slope out the back door. My stomach's doing somersaults, and mam looks shaken but not like she's going to cry.

Ruth glances over her shoulder at us, but her usual expression has changed. I have a rush of pity because she's drawn the short straw and she knows it. It's one thing leaving your husband, but I wonder how a mam can leave her child like hers did. Perhaps she felt the nastiness in her like me, or perhaps that was the price she had to pay for getting away from her husband's clutches.

When they're over the threshold, Mam shuts the kitchen door after them and locks it, securing the bolts just to be sure. She lifts up the curtains to check they're out of the gate and I think there'll be plenty of others in town doing the same tonight. Brian and Ruth will be doing the walk of shame, but it could have been more shameful. He's had a let off and he'll realise it when he's had chance to think about it.

"Tea, toast?" mam asks, leaning against the door. She looks as drained as I feel. Part of me wants to put the day behind us, to go to bed and wake up when it's a new start, but then I remember I haven't eaten since this morning.

Nodding, I give her a weary half smile.

I head into the front room like I'm sleepwalking to bank up the fire for us. Mam told me on that terrible day in December, you feel colder when you've had a shock. She brings the tray in, and we settle ourselves down in our natural spots, our natural places of safety. Spearing the bread on the long fork I hold it to the fire. We have a toaster, but this makes it better by a mile. I start to calm down as the bread steadily colours to the right shade of golden. I smother it in butter whilst it's still hot.

Silently we devour the simple pleasure of hot, buttered toast like it's the finest feast, and this time we eat and enjoy every last scrap.

Afterwards, mam sits back and smiles across at me, and I know she's thinking the same as me: that it's lovely it's just the two of us.

"I never thought today would end like this. I thought we'd all be celebrating the wedding at the club tonight," she says.

We sit staring into the fire for a while and I start thinking about what would happen to mam when we got back from celebrating. Stop it, Dolly, I think, that's all in the past now, so there's no point stewing. It doesn't quite feel real yet that we're rid of all that.

I look down and notice I'm still wearing my bridesmaid dress and mam's still sitting in her finery but it's too late in the day to change now. I very much doubt Ruth will have taken her dress with her so it will probably be hanging upstairs when I go up. I like the thought of having my bedroom back to myself again, it's more than a nice thought. My stomach starts to settle properly, and I feel the peace I used to before dad died. Except, as mam said that time, I wasn't aware of feeling peaceful then. It's funny how you have to lose something to know the value of it.

It's also funny, I think how a man has the power to make you happy or miserable. Mam has had a taste of both now. The problem is that although I had my worries which I tried and failed to keep to myself, we never knew what Brian was really like until he got the ring on mam's finger. He was always so charming to anybody who was of use to him. He had everybody fooled but me, but then, like Mrs Turrell, I wasn't any use to him.

I think of Margaret and wish as I do every single day, she was still here. That I could head a few doors down and just sit with her and have the comfort of her quietness. Part of me thought they might all want to come back home to Wakeley when she got well but I would never ask the question because that's none of my business. Perhaps the house they live in now has become their home.

Margaret told me when dad died that out of every bad thing which happens you should think about what you'd learned from it to help you get over it.

It took me a long time to think of something after we lost dad forever. I couldn't bring to mind anything of worth which I'd learned for ages. In the end, I decided I'd learned that life goes on even without someone you can't imagine having to live your life without. At the time it didn't seem much, especially as Brian and Ruth were dragging us down, making our new life almost unbearable.

Now I'd learned so much, even over the last eight hours. I'd learned that Mrs Turrell is kinder than she appears, that badness gets found out in the end, and that my mother is a force to be reckoned with when she's pushed to the limit.

But the main thing I'd been thinking about late at night over the last three years, is something which wouldn't be leaving me in a hurry.

I learned I wouldn't be taking such a chance on any bloke.

Not if it bloody killed me.

Chapter 10
Harriet Then

I love Dolly Hunter.

She doesn't care or even know, but I do.

I've never met her, but I can picture her well enough. I never met mum either, but grandpa's stories make them both appear clear and bright in my mind. I always wonder if I didn't have those stories, would they still look the same or different to me when I conjure up their images, which I find myself doing often.

The first time I really got to know Dolly Hunter properly was on my thirteenth birthday. That day I was old enough to realise for the first time you didn't have to spend a lot of money to make a special memory. My friends who go on their foreign holidays every year might not agree but they're the ones who are missing out most. They don't brag about their lives because they feel sorry for me. There's no need but I don't mind because if you feel sorry for someone it means you're a kind person. I value kindness above all else in life.

Grandpa had taken the day off for my birthday and we'd gone to the park on the other side of Stainton. I was a little old to go to the park, but I would never have told him. We needed to get the bus, then walk over the bridge but when you got to the other side, it was grass like a carpet as he called it. Even the high-rise flats as a backdrop didn't spoil the view, in fact I liked the contrast of town and parkland. We had sandwiches wrapped in foil and hot, sugary tea from a flask. Gran didn't come but I didn't expect her to. It hurts to think about it now, but if I'm being totally honest, if she'd come, I don't think I would have had my special memory.

We bought a cake from the supermarket on the way back to the bus. There were fancy ones, but I picked a lemon cake as it's always been our favourite.

"You don't need to go for the cheapest, I know you. It's your birthday," grandpa told me, but I really would have picked it anyway.

When we got back, gran was still upstairs. The house was chilly, so I put the heating on and then the gas fire in the kitchen, while grandpa nipped to see her. I unwrapped the fish and chips we'd bought from *Bailey's* and placed half of my fish and a few chips on a plate with a cup of tea. Grandpa stepped to one side on the landing when he saw me with the tray.

I didn't ask how gran was because I knew.

Her cough had worsened over the previous couple of years. We'd taken her for a chest x-ray more than once and there was scarring on her lungs but whatever was wrong wasn't "significant or urgent" grandpa told me. I memorised the words because they were so strange. He thought they were strange too and he wished he'd asked more but he was just so relieved it wasn't the worst thing he was expecting to hear. She'd taken to sleeping most of the day and pacing all night, smoking cigarettes one after another so when I came down it was my first job to empty the ashtray. I hated the stale smell it left hanging in the air and how it made the walls so yellowy brown, that we had to paint them every year. Nobody else I know smokes anymore and I know I never will.

Gran was curled up on top of their flowery duvet, staring out the window. Her short grey hair was matted at the back where she'd been laid for hours staring at the ceiling. She will have turned over when she heard me coming up the stairs, like she always did but she didn't think I realised. The pills on the bedside table were lined up as neatly as I'd left them, and I spotted the full ashtray to take back down with me. I was always scared of her smoking in bed, but she said she was careful never to fall asleep. She needed a shower, I remembered. Grandpa said he'd get her to have one later as we needed to get off early for my birthday to make the best of the weather.

"Teatime, gran," I said cheerfully, putting the tray on the opposite side of the bed, "leave what you can't eat."

That's what I said every time.

"Thanks, love, I'll have it in a minute."

That's what she said every time. Sometimes she ate more than others, sometimes the ate nothing at all.

She carried on staring out of the window and I walked round to stroke her hair back from her face. Smiling down at her she looked up and gave me a weak one in return. It looked such an effort.

"A shower for you in a bit, Mrs H, don't think we've forgotten," I joked.

She tugged at my cardigan which was dangling in front of her face.

"No peace for the wicked with you two," she jostled back at me.

"See you in a bit then," I said, but she'd gone back in her own world already. I'd grown used to it; she could never manage to stay long.

In the kitchen, grandpa had the table laid with a tablecloth, and the cake with the candle was waiting in the middle.

"Well, I don't know where the last thirteen years have gone, Hattie," he told me, shaking his head in disbelief when we sat down, "but I feel like we've had you forever. You're an old head on young shoulders, there's no mistaking it," he swallowed, so I felt slightly alarmed, "but then I suppose you've not had a lot of choice."

I quickly gave him a big smile and told him to get on with the best fish and chips in town before they got cold.

He laughed because he always called them that. He still does.

We usually eat them out of the paper because they taste nicer, but he always makes a special effort for my birthday.

After he cleared the plates away, he lit the candle on my cake and sang happy birthday in an operatic voice to make me laugh. We'd been to the playhouse once to see the opera. We might have picked the wrong one, grandpa thought because we found *Sweeney Todd* a little on the dull side.

"Heck, I thought they were going to sing a song about washing the pots," he laughed when we came out, "but you have to try everything once. What's the point of having all this culture on tap if we're not going to engage with it?"

He sat back down in his chair and handed me a tiny gift bag he'd hidden under the table. I thanked him with my biggest smile.

"Don't look so delighted, you don't know what it is yet," he joked, but he knew I'd be happy with anything he got me. I could imagine him going into a shop and awkwardly trying to pick something for a young girl. It made my heart flip to think about it.

Inside the bag was a small box. When I opened the spring lid, I jumped up from my chair to hug him with excitement. It was a pair of teeny gold hoop earrings. I knew how much thought had gone into them.

My friend Charlotte who I walked to school with, had her ears pierced earlier that year and she told us all about it. I wanted mine piercing so badly when I saw her earrings, but I didn't like to ask. Grandpa must have realised what I was thinking. How sweet he was to remember.

"You can walk into town at the weekend and get them done with Charlotte as she knows the drill."

"Oh, grandpa, thank you so much," I said, staring at the earrings in wonder, and I felt the same about the person who bought them for me, "I can't believe you remembered."

I looked up to see him grinning at me, fair bursting with pride.

"Come on, Hattie, leave all this, let's sit by the fire in the front room before I go up to see your gran. I have something else for you, and I've been waiting for the right time. I think on balance, thirteen is just about right."

I felt strange. Not excited, just odd as it didn't sound entirely like he was offering me a gift. Following him down the tiled passage we headed to the best room, as I still think of it. We never went in there except Christmas Day as the kitchen's big enough to live in. The house is huge; old but huge. It's a house from money, grandpa told me, and you can tell. The hall has a sweeping staircase, with a polished dark wood stair rail and the beautiful blue, cream and brown patterned tiles go all the way from the front to the back door. I mop them every Saturday morning, thinking about how many other people will have done them before me. We have a cellar and an attic which run the whole length of the house and the master bedroom has an en-suite originally installed in the 1930s. There's a servant's board in the cellar with a bell for each room and the boy scouts used to hold meetings in there for a year or so. They were no trouble, and so grateful to have somewhere to meet while the Institute was being refurbished.

The house has been let by a private landlord since the sixties, but between us we keep up to it. We have a back yard with an outside toilet that we now use as a little potting shed with a shiny red door.

There's an old pub opposite us called *The Crown* and grandpa slopes off every once in a while, for a "swift half", as he calls it. I can see him from my bedroom window, sitting with the regulars. He's never without company, whatever time he goes. I tell him he should go more often because he always looks happy when I see him through the window, but then he says it wouldn't be a treat.

In the best room, I watched grandpa lighting the fire. He didn't even use firelighters, just newspaper, kindling and matches, yet he had it going in no time. I was getting nearly as good; I knew because he timed me sometimes.

"I have a few more years of practice under my belt," he laughed, when I couldn't quite beat him.

We could have had a gas fire installed like we did in the kitchen, but he says the real fire reminds him of home, proper home. I'm glad he's kept it.

We waited for the fire to take hold properly and I was thinking the whole time about what he was going to give me. I couldn't even imagine.

Eventually he made his way to the wooden dresser with an oval mirror in the back, which is still next to the window. I love that dresser, it's so classy. It was in the house when we moved in, along with a piano. They would have been old fashioned in the sixties but now everybody wants them again.

He pulled a box from the second drawer. As he looked at it for too long, I could tell he was still in two minds if it was the right time to hand it over. He made his final decision and came back to sit down in the chair opposite. The street was quiet and without the television, I had the feeling you get when it's like you're the only people in the world.

"Your dad gave me these a long time ago and I've often laid awake wondering when the right time would be to give them to you, if at all. I haven't read them, and I don't want to upset you, lass, but I think you're old enough now to make that decision for yourself."

I stared at the jewellery box. I wasn't sure if I'd like what was inside, by the way grandpa was talking. But more, because of the expression on his face.

I took the box from him after a while and placed it on my knee. I was beyond curious by then, but I didn't want to rush. Opening it up slowly I saw some rings and necklaces, twinkling on the black velvet lining of the top compartment. I knew immediately they must have been mums. There was a wedding and engagement ring and one with diamonds clustered together in the shape of a heart. There was a gold lady's watch and a man's watch, but they didn't match. I ran my fingers over all the items, taking in their fine detail.

"They're beautiful," I said.

"They are, that," he answered, "the man's watch was your dad's that your other gran wanted me to have as your other grandpa had already died. I placed it in there for safe keeping."

His voice sounded crackly, so he cleared his throat.

"I wish your gran could be here to do this with me, but you know she's not herself and that's all there is to it," he took a deep breath, "if you lift up the top tray, there's something underneath."

I carried on looking at the rings and watches for a moment then I peeped under the tray. I saw a pile of letters, wrapped in a lilac ribbon. Picking them out carefully I put the box on the table and replaced it with the letters on my lap. I sat staring at them a moment. When I looked up at grandpa, he was staring at them as intently as I was.

I waited for him to speak for a while, then he said, "I've told you about your mum's best friend in Wakeley called Dolly."

I nod. I've always loved the name.

"Well, when we left, they wrote to each other for a time, until well, until they couldn't. I would never throw them away so, here they are. If you don't want to read them, you don't have to, but I think it's only right you have them."

He sat back in his chair, seeming relieved he'd made a decision. I felt like I'd been handed a box of lost treasure and I suppose the letters are just that in a way.

"Well, whether I read them or not, I'll look after them, grandpa. I'll make sure I look after them forever, don't look so worried."

I meant it.

"I know you will, lass and I'm glad you've got them now."

He settled back in his chair, and I tucked the letters back in the box then placed it on the side table. As we sat together chatting then watching television, my eyes kept going to the box, I couldn't help it.

After an hour or so, the clock chimed eight times and I stood up, eager to go upstairs for once. I was trying my best to hide the fact.

"Tea?" I asked, knowing the answer already.

"I'll bring you and your gran one up, then get her sorted."

I smiled then kissed his cheek.

"It's been the best birthday, grandpa. I'm so grateful for all the trouble you went to."

He patted my hand on his shoulder.

"You're no bother Hattie, and I don't know what your gran and me would do without you."

A shadow of guilt passed over his face but then he smiled quickly up at me to hide it.

When I went up to see gran, I left the box on the landing table because I didn't want her to see it. She was sitting up in bed in the darkness with her tray to one side, more or less exactly as I'd left.

"You've done well with that, gran," I said like she was a little child, "you must have been hungry."

I went to kiss her goodnight and held my breath, so I didn't have to smell her. I felt terrible but I always did that.

I couldn't place the smell as she showered every day, but I think now it was the smell of someone who had given up. To me, it was a sign of her sadness.

"Night, Hattie," she said.

"Night gran. Grandpa is on his way up."

I swooped up the box then opened the bottle green door to climb another set of stairs to my room in the attic. It's the biggest one in the house so I'm lucky to have it. I've got a second-hand sofa, a small tv, a desk to do my homework and a cd player to listen to music. It's my own little world and I've never minded my own company. I'm not a great talker but I'm thankful because my natural instinct is to smile, so it stops me from appearing standoffish. Grandpa says I'm like him, preferring to keep my thoughts in check by being busy and looking on the bright side. It works for him, and it works for me.

After saying goodnight to grandpa, I flopped myself on the sofa and put the cd which was already in the player on low. Carole King started singing from where she had left off. My friends still think I've got a strange taste in music, but I like old music as well as the new bands. They said it was strange but kind of cool too. Music is still a big part of me. I was in the school choir, and I often catch myself singing when I don't realise.

"I've never known anybody sound as happy as you while they're working. Well, not in real life anyway," grandpa said once, laughing at me.

The intricate jewellery box which keeps the letters safe is black with a glossy lacquer and Korean houses painted on the top. An orange tassel lets you pull up the top layer inside and there's a miniature tassel on the tiny key. My gran has a similar one on her dressing table and she told me grandpa brought three back from Korea when he was stationed there during his National Service; one for her, one for his mum and one for his sister. I always wondered where the others had got to.

I took out the letters taking great care not to tear them, then untied the lilac ribbon. I meticulously unfolded each one and placed them on my small table in date order. It didn't take long because only two were out of sync. The writing was old-style but not as fancy as gran and grandpas and the paper had been torn from a wire-bound notepad.

I looked at the last letter on top of the pile. For some reason, this letter was drawing me the most as I thought it was the last real glimpse of mum and her best friend. Picking the letter up I drew my legs under me on the settee in my favourite position to get comfortable.

It was dated 11th February 1985. That was the year before I was born, I thought briefly.

The letter read:

Dear Margaret,
I'm glad you've settled into your lovely new house.
You and Ronnie look very happy stood outside it in the photograph you sent me. I'm going to put it in a frame when I get round to it.
After all you went through to get well, I bet you never imagined getting married and buying a house! I bet your

mam and dad are chuffed to bits. It will give your mam a lift, I hope, as you said she'd been a bit low.

My news is that I've just got a raise from Lumley's so I'm managing to put some money by at last. Mam's taking things a bit easier after her hysterectomy and I'm glad because she's always done too much.

We also got some sad news that Ralph's gran passed away. It got me thinking about all that kerfuffle at the wedding that never was. I still have no idea where Ralph got to but fancy him coming back a hero in the end rather than with his tail between his legs. I see him about a lot and he's still popular with all the girls in town. He's no idea and I think that's what makes him even more popular. He got a promotion so he's a gaffer now at Worthies and was even voted in as union rep not long back. I imagine he's got a lot on his plate with the changes that are taking place there at the minute. I keep hearing plenty of mumblings and grumblings, but it's been there nearly a hundred years, so I'm sure it'll see me out.

I know I say it every time in one way or another, but I miss not being able to nip down to yours for a natter even now. When I got my raise, I wanted to tell you and that's happened many times over the years.

I'm going to try and catch the post, so I'll sign off now, but I'll look forward to your next letter when you get chance.

Love Dolly x

So, that was the day I fell in love with Dolly Hunter. She felt like an extension of my mum which gave me a feeling I'd never experienced before: a feeling of comfort.

I folded the letters back up, retied the bow then placed them back in the jewellery box to read them all another time.

I know them off by heart now.

It's always a pleasure to think back to one of my special memories, thanks to grandpa and to Dolly Hunter.

I now realise gran feels worse on my birthday because this is also the day when she lost my mum forever. I also now realise she's doing her best to be with her but grandpa and me, keep pulling her back so she's trapped in limbo between both worlds.

Grandpa explained to me once that a few weeks after mum died, my dad 'died from a broken heart'. I thought it sounded so romantic.

But I'm old enough now to know what this really means.

Chapter 11
Harriet Now

Aside from a touch of bird muck on the ampersand, the words could have been carved in the stone and placed in their prime position yesterday.

Thos Worthington & Sons – Est 1894, it reads.

Simple yet effective, always the best way, as Ralph would say. I turn and look at the view of the building, seeing the warts and all of the town, the snow a poor camouflage. Regardless, the town and its people haven't lost any of their copper soul; I can still see it clearly, though I might be in a minority.

I stand on my tiptoes to try and see through one of the small panes of glass in the bottom right window. The wet condensation means I need to wipe a hole with my hand, but then I see the machines sitting just as they might have in 1894. Preserved in time, like a village fleeing a radioactive explosion or a volcano. Aside that is, from the layer of filth and cobwebs. The eeriness of the memories inside creeps over me, making me shiver.

Stepping backwards I crane my neck to study the vastness of the silhouette, the two tall chimneys poking upwards from the rear of the building. Only one of them is still complete but it's still a steadfast monument to a moment in time. A time when it was that shining copper soul of the town, giving focus and meaning to the lives of hundreds of families. Like copper itself, it may become tarnished when left to its own devices, but the strength remains intact always.

The new copper works in Stainton was an ugly blot on the landscape, entirely fit for purpose. This building even now has industrial grandeur, a kind of utilitarian beauty.

Ralph told me it was cheaper to buy new machinery than move it. The council bought the land and keep it more or less in one piece because they're worried about it becoming a drug den or a squat. I laughed at that. I can't imagine there's many druggies in Wakeley.

As I head back down the hill to the church, I scan the rows of houses and imagine them as they once were. I picture line after line of Dolly's house, standing tall and proud side by side, the chimney's releasing some of the warmth inside towards the dark winter sky. It was a reality not so very long ago.

I smile to myself. Dolly has not been what I expected. She definitely isn't the person I drew in my mind from the tone of the letters; the girly chatter between best friends was misleading. To be fair to Dolly though, I'm a complete stranger and they were written in another age. At first, I thought I would just tell her who I was and make it easier for myself but, as I told Ralph, I want her to like me for me, not my family. That might have been a mistake, however well-intentioned. She's a hard taskmaster but I know one thing, the Dolly of today would expect her trust to be earned. It's proving difficult to budge the armour, but I somehow still can't help but find it an admirable trait.

I turn off the road into the woods and spot the church at the back of the gravestones. Some of the stones are grand and ornate, some less so, depending on the owner's standing in the community. I had no idea such a thing existed as a tin church, so this was a charming surprise.

"Mum," Lydia shouts as she bounds through the snow to greet me, "Mr Ralph says he's got a team! I can play football again."

I hunker down to pull her into my arms, sharing her delight. She's missed the thrill of a game, I know that. It feels good to soak up her joy for a second.

"You've certainly made a little girl very happy," I tell Ralph.

He smiles at me over his shoulder as he locks the church shed. Lydia's been helping him with his odd jobs as the snow doesn't stop him or anyone else here from getting on with life.

"Come and have some dinner with us if you've got time," I say.

"Now that's something I've got in abundance, although not so much nowadays."

He laughs, tickling Lydia under the chin so she chuckles and wriggles away.

I listen to them chatting like old friends in the front room while I plate up the shepherds' pie I've had on a low heat. Lydia's sitting on the rug by the coffee table, playing with her large dolls head on a stand which she calls Daisy.

Ralph's half-watching the rugby on the tv. I love that she's a contradiction, that she's a tomboy but still loves everything girlie. The house is clean and snug already. Every room has been freshly painted over the last few weeks, and I bought a small stash of coal from Sally Evans until I get a big delivery. The company only deliver once a month Ralph told me, and he's already rung through my order. How marvellous he's been.

After dinner at the table, I take the wine through to the front room.

"I don't really drink in the house," Ralph says, holding his glass up, "it's not good to drink alone, they say. I've never had much red wine before but it's quite pleasant. Better with food, maybe."

"Quite the connoisseur, Kellett," I laugh.

He snorts.

"Oh, aye."

"I think I'm going to ask Mrs Dolly if she'll let me do her hair and makeup one time," Lydia says, skilfully applying eyeshadow to Daisy for about the third time today.

I look over her head at Ralph and we grimace then grin, sharing the joke.

"I'd like to be here when you ask her that one," Ralph says.

He sits forward in his chair all set to go home.

"Well, I'll not outstay my welcome," he says, "I'll let you ladies get on and thank you kindly for your hospitality."

Lydia shoots a look his way.

"Don't go yet," she says, her expression almost panic-stricken.

She loves company. We've never had much of it before for one reason or another.

Ralph looks my way shyly. This man is so endearing with his quiet charm, I think yet again.

"You're more than welcome to stay a while. Lydia's going to bed soon and I'd love to hear some tales of old Wakeley. I bet you could write a book having lived here so many years."

"I'd like to hear them too," Lydia pipes up.

"I tell you what," I say, "why doesn't Mr Ralph read you a story after your bath while I'm washing up. If he doesn't mind, of course."

His face tells me he doesn't mind at all.

"That will make a right nice change," he says, smiling at me like I've handed him a gift with a bow on top.

I feel like I have.

*

"How long were you married?" I ask Ralph, pulling the throw around me to get settled on the sofa.

He puts his cup on the coffee table and sits back in the chair.

"In the end, about six weeks," he chuckles but I was a lot longer getting shut of her. I married on the rebound, except there wasn't much bounding from Dolly's so-called stepsister, Ruth. I was never that taken with her, but she was keen, and I was gormless enough to go along with her railroading me into her wedding plans. I left mam, dad, and gran a note on the dresser to tell them I couldn't go through with the wedding but not to worry about me and I'd be in touch when I got myself settled. When I wrote to my mam a few months later and she wrote back telling me about the drama, I had to come back. I knew then it wouldn't upset the applecart for Dolly and her mam. I just had to come home and tell the truth. Before I left, I thought they'd hate me for what I'd done to Ruth as they seemed such a happy little family. But I couldn't go through with the wedding."

I knew some of this from grandpa, but I'm keen to hear Ralph's story straight from the horse's mouth.

"It must have been hard for you, discovering the truth."

"It was, and when I got back and told Joan and Dolly, I thought they'd be delighted and they were, but they'd changed. The damage had been done and the justice didn't seem to soften them much. They were always kind-hearted and would give anyone their last tanner, but they weren't the same Joan and Dolly I'd left behind."

He looks wistfully into the fire, and I think quickly how to lighten the mood.

"So, you came back a hero and got your job back at *Worthington's,* for a time at least."

"I did, and it was good while it lasted."

"When I was looking at the old building today, I could see it all in my mind, the hard graft, the banter, the friendships. I find it fascinating that it was so important to Wakeley for so long."

"Well, I suppose we have to thank Thomas Worthington for that. The original one, mind, not the one I knew. He had a vision ahead of his time and I can imagine there were many who thought he was barmy. He was from money, and of course he wanted to build a successful business, but it was important to him to share the benefits of its success with the people of Wakeley. I suppose you could say he wanted to look after their health and wellbeing and give them a life very different to working down the pit. He built a school, a church, a social club, and his workers respected him and more importantly, thrived. I wish I'd met him. I used to look at his photograph on the wall of the club and think how hard it would have been to sell his vision to the shareholders in that day and age, how much opposition he would have needed to overcome."

Ralph has wandered back into that old world as he pauses and takes a sip of his tea. I stay silent; I don't want to stem his flow after waiting to so long to hear his tales.

"Anyway, when he had a son and they were old enough, he insisted they didn't just take a role in the office, he wanted them to work their way up, starting as an apprentice. He was clever enough to know that way the workers would carry on the respect they had for him and the copperworks would continue to go from strength to strength with each generation. People don't realise how much money could be made in copper back then.

I was working with the fourth generation Thomas Worthington who was older than me, but he'd done his apprenticeship, worked on the shop floor and then he went on to learning the ropes from his father. I'd heard from the old-timers that the one before him wasn't as amenable, but our Thomas was a good bloke, almost one of us as far as he could be anyway. He'd join us for a pint at Christmas and watch us play rugby even though he struggled with the Rugby League rules, him being a Rugby Union man, having gone to a private school. We always had his ear and when Dolly's dad was killed, he made sure they were set up even though the accident had cost him a fortune in repairs and loss of earnings. He was one of the good ones; still is as far as I know.

I went on to be made foreman and then the blokes voted me in as shop steward. It was only a token gesture, more a feather in your cap than anything else as we didn't really need one. Or we didn't need a shop steward right up until we did. They were good days, Hattie. I like to think of them as the glory days."

I nod. Grandpa has told me plenty about Wakeley over the years, but I really can imagine because they both bring it to life for me.

"Wakeley copper tubing and fittings were the best in the world, no doubt about it. But times change, and of course nothing lasts forever, even though you think it will.

Copper use was diversifying; telecommunications was the next big thing and there was good money to be made in it.

Business is first and foremost about money and it just didn't make good business sense to keep Wakeley going. It was chosen as the site for the copper works because it was near to the coal needed to power the boilers, but the pits were all closing, and they needed to make the switch to gas. They needed bigger premises to meet modern health and safety rules; we all found out the hard way what a death-trap these old three-storey factories can be. Land was going cheap on the outskirts of Leeds and Thomas Worthington realised it was cheaper to build a new plant than try and breathe life into this one.

To be fair to him, he wanted to take everyone with him and recreate what we had here over there and even employ more staff. But we were having none of it. Aside from the odd time visiting sick family, and my short trip to pastures new, the majority of us hadn't stepped foot beyond Thorndale, never mind tipping our lives up to head to the big city. Forward-thinking and well-meaning or not, we felt betrayed. More, we felt Thomas Worthington of all people was the one who was betraying us.

I went to meeting after meeting to plead our case, but I know now I was wasting my breath, not because Thomas was being awkward but because *Worthington's* would have gone under anyway if they hadn't diversified. He told me enough times, but I wasn't listening, none of us were.

We're proud, principled folk for all the good it did us back then."

He runs his fingers through his hair, and I can clearly see the pain the memory causes him etched in every crease of his face. To live with regret is the worst pain of all I know that. The townsfolk have paid a heavy price for their principles.

"I'm ashamed to say one of the last conversations I had with Thomas was an unpleasant one. I'd had enough of listening to him telling me the town wouldn't survive without the copperworks, that we'd be shooting ourselves in the foot if we didn't follow him. I just snapped.

It was the end of another long meeting with both of us saying the same things. I was frustrated and I got up to leave, storming my way towards the door. I could sense him watching me.

I can picture myself now, standing with the brass knob in my hand then turning my head and saying, "There are those who wish you were on the other side of the door that day in December, instead of Eric Hunter, you know."

He looked like I'd punched him in the stomach. I didn't care at that moment I'd done that to him. I've had many more moments since where I've felt differently about it.

"And are you saying you're one of them, Ralph?" he asked me.

I stared at him, and I can imagine the venom on my own face, staring back at him. I shouldn't have said it in the first place, but then I should have taken my chance to say I wasn't one of them because I wasn't. But I was young, angry, and stubborn, a lethal combination. I just turned on my heel, barged out the door and slammed it behind me. That must have hurt him bad. I didn't even apologise the day after when I'd cooled off a bit, and I regret that more. He had the town's interest at heart I know that now, I've known it a long, long time but then hindsight's a wonderful thing."

His head hangs and I can't bear it. I go over to kneel at his feet and put my hands over his. He swallows more than once but won't look at me.

"I left to work at *Lumley's* before *Worthies* closed down for good two years later. Dolly told me about a job, and I grabbed the opportunity before anyone else as I'd got my mam to think of then. About half the town had the good sense to follow him and we felt more let down by them than Thomas.

Of course, reality sank in quickly. They'd been given a pay-out and the retired folk lived on their pensions. A few managed to get a job at *Lumley's* or in Thorndale, but they were in the minority. Slowly the other families were forced to leave to look for work. Nobody came to replace them; why would they? What do we have to offer a family?

The last thing Thomas Worthington did was put the brass plaque up for Dolly's dad next to the church door. He did it on the quiet the night before he left. It was a measure of the man he was… the man he is."

Ralph's bottom lip trembles but he does his best to shake off his distress with a small smile. Our hands are still joined but he doesn't pull them away.

"Anyway, enough about me, I've been thinking you must be missing your grandpa and Dan. Have they any plans to join you?"

I get to my feet and head back over to the settee, trying to pull my mind away from old Wakeley to the Wakeley of today. I don't want to talk about me; I could listen to Ralph for hours.

I'm thinking it was an appropriate but kind gesture on Thomas's part to provide a commemoration plaque for Dolly's dad after all the upset and the town hating what he himself stood for. Progress was not on the townsfolks' list of priorities because progress meant unwanted and drastic change. You couldn't blame them; they couldn't understand the situation needed fixing because they didn't know it was on the way to being broken. They didn't have the foresight. It wasn't broken then.

My mind goes fleetingly now to Ruth's part in all this. Thank goodness she spilled the beans to Ralph when she'd had one too many on the run up to the wedding. It sounds like he had a lucky escape.

Poor Joan and Dolly, you can only imagine. You can only imagine the shame they had to live with all those years, thinking Eric had started the fire that day in December. When all along it was that nasty piece of work, Brian Addlebury.

Chapter 12
Harriet Then

    Now and again, I wish I came home to a warm house. I don't want much; I just wish there was somebody there to ask me if I'd had a good day and perhaps sit and have a cup of tea with me. Grandpa always asks me when he gets home of course but sometimes, not often, I wish it was different. It's usually when the weather's particularly cold or if it's been raining all day. I know I'll get in and the house will be damp and unwelcoming. I'll have to make gran a drink and a sandwich which she barely touches and head upstairs in my coat. The house takes ages to get warm because it's old with high ceilings, but gran doesn't feel cold under the bedcovers.

    I hang my bag on the back of the chair and put the kettle on. I flick the heating switch then suddenly hear a loud thud coming from upstairs. I stop in my tracks. Gran's fallen again, I know the familiar sound, which will make it twice this week. Her cough is enough to wake the dead, but we've given up trying to persuade her to go to hospital again, it only makes her too distressed.

    Snapping my brain into action I run up the stairs and push the bedroom door open so quickly it bangs back against the wall. The sound of it startles me then the silence afterwards is unsettling. The duvet cover is back and gran's nowhere in sight. She must have gone to the bathroom, there's nowhere else she would venture.

As I push the door to the en-suite, I can feel a resistance behind it. I know immediately who it is.

"Gran, can you move just a little so I can get in?" I ask, my level tone betraying the panic I'm feeling inside.

The silence continues.

I push the door again and it opens an inch. She's no weight so I keep going gently but firmly and manage eventually to get over the threshold.

I see her contorted body first. Her head is back and there's still a light in her eyes. The barest of lights. I sink to the floor and gather her into my arms, cradling her tiny head on my knees. I have the overpowering desperation of wanting to keep her here, with me, with us. I don't want her to go. Oh gran, please don't leave us.

Too fast my hope fades.

I watch on helplessly as the light floats from her brown eyes for good. I watch the shift from life to death. The moment I've imagined a thousand times has finally arrived, it's here. Except it's not like I imagined at all.

Pushing her hair from her face I stroke it backwards, over and over again, remembering how I used to set it for her once a week to keep it tidy. That was when she could be bothered. When she hadn't given in.

Tears drip from my face onto hers as I trace a finger around it, wanting to seal every inch in my mind for all time. I'm to blame for wishing things were different sometimes, I think.

From nowhere a feeling appears. I'm suddenly flooded with a need to make her comfortable. She shouldn't be laying undignified on the floor for a second longer. She's heavier in death than in life, so I need to part carry, part pull her to the bed and lift her onto it. I tuck the duvet up and under her chin like she's a sick child and sit on the edge of the bed. I comb her hair, so she looks more like my old gran then I sit very still watching her. We stay together this way for a long time, perhaps longer than we should.

I don't want to make the call to grandpa. I don't want to have the police come, or the ambulance or both. I don't want her to be taken away forever on a stretcher and then think about the funeral arrangements. I'm so tired, and I could lay down beside her and go to sleep. I'm not scared by that thought at all for some reason.

But I do go downstairs to make the call and the ball starts rolling to take us to another phase of our life. One without gran. The situation may have been far from perfect, but gran was my normality. She was my focus.

She was grandpa's focus before mine. I've often imagined them when they were going out and when they got married. I've seen black and white photographs of gran in a fitted white dress and veil she borrowed from her friend. Her waist tiny and her shiny black hair up in a comb slide on both sides of her head. Grandpa in his suit looking tall and impressive, his hair which I know was dark red like mine, in film star waves, as gran called them.

Her stoic protector then and always.

I want to find a man like grandpa one day, one who honours his vows not through duty, but because the love remained throughout terrible times. It's been tested more than most I would think. They had a sick daughter they lost and a son-in-law who followed her soon afterwards. They had to start their life again away from a town which was home to make sure their child had the best chance, but she died anyway. They had to raise an orphan granddaughter as their own.

It was cruel because gran was so fragile as grandpa always described her and was it any wonder?

Fragile she may have been, I think but she was always in good hands.

*

It surprises me when ten people including the vicar, grandpa, and me attend gran's funeral. The other six are neighbours and the seventh is someone who grandpa works with called Barry. He never met gran.

Sometimes people attend funerals to support the living rather than mourn the dead, grandpa told me. We set the time for two o'clock, one of the decisions we made without rhyme or reason, just because we had to.

Everyone comes back to the house for a sandwich and a glass of sherry afterwards. I force small-talk, and they end up chatting amongst themselves for a while because they know each other well by the sound of it. I want them to go but I keep filling up their plates politely, keeping busy, waiting it out.

When the clock on the mantle strikes four times, Barry gets up to make a move which prompts everyone else. Oh, the relief.

After thanking them all for coming and their good wishes, we shut the door and head into the kitchen to do the washing up.

"Well, it helps to get that over with," grandpa says, folding the tea towel and hanging it on the cooker rail, "it's the best and the worst ritual we created for ourselves, but now we have, they must be observed."

"Yes, it was kind of them all to make the effort and the vicar really tried his best with the eulogy when we could offer so little about gran's life."

I thought it was a lesson to be learned.

As I make my way into the front room, I'm thinking about the few changes we've made already in the ten days since we lost gran. We use this room every night and the kitchens just for cooking and eating now we've decided. It's a beautiful front room and a shame only to use it for high days and holidays. It seems an awful lot can happen in ten days.

The tv's on low but neither of us are watching. Grandpa broddles the fire back to life then sits back down in his chair. I can sense he's working up to something as he seems quiet and pensive.

"I've been sorting a few things out Hattie to keep my mind busy, as you know."

I nod but now I'm pensive. I've seen brown envelopes arriving and papers piled on the kitchen table for days, needing to move them when we eat. I realise changes are obviously afoot and they can't all be for the better.

"The main thing I want to talk to you about is our finances. We've needed to be careful with money, but your gran and I took out life insurance years ago. It's worth a tidy sum now she's … not here."

The stumble over his words makes my throat tighten. I never cry unless I'm in bed because I hate the thought of upsetting him. I suspect he does the same. His face is taut now, so I'm struggling to keep my emotions in check.

"Well, the upshot is I've been thinking of our futures as you might imagine. I've decided I'm going to finish work and have more time at home. I've needed to work a bit longer than I'd have liked but now I don't have to."

"I can't lie, I'm delighted," I say, relieved that I won't have to be on my own in the house quite so much. Gran may not have been much company, but the house never felt empty like it has over the last ten days.

He clears his throat.

"Aye, well the other thing is, I've been thinking about it a lot and I'd like it if you went to university, now we've got the money."

I open my mouth, but he puts his hand up.

"Now, don't say anything until I've finished, love if you don't mind. You've always been clever, and your gran and I had been putting some savings by before this happened. She wasn't always as bad as she was towards the end, and we used to have plenty of discussions about your future. You know how she loved you and she couldn't help how she was."

He stops to take a breath and I look down at my hands.

"Anyway, we would have been over the moon if your mother had been well enough to have the opportunities you could have. I've been to enough meetings at school to know how well you're doing, and you're destined for good things, anyone with half a mind can see that. All I ask is that you think about it but know this: I can't imagine a single thing I'd rather spend the money on."

I'm aghast; in all my born days, I never thought university would be an option for me.

I look over at my grandpa still in his black tie loosened since our guest left, his grey hair waving from his forehead. He's been my whole world, my whole life. Mother, father, grandmother, grandfather, best friend, mentor, soulmate. I can't even consider going away We need each other more than ever now, I think. The fact he's prepared to let me live away when he needs me the most just so I can have the best opportunities makes the gesture all the more special.

I must choose my next words carefully.

"I will give it some thought," I say, though perhaps I'm not being entirely honest, "but I'm happy to start at the bottom and work my way up like we've always spoken about. I remember your tales about the Worthington's and how much respect they earned doing just that."

We smile at each other, recalling the memories.

"That may be, but some shrouded opportunities come at the right time for the right reason, and you should bear that in mind before you decide anything for definite. You've time to think about it and you should take it."

I know he's right. I've always wanted to be a solicitor; it's more than just a career choice. I won't just dismiss it, I think, it obviously means a lot to him and perhaps I could go to university in the city and then I don't have to move away.

I tell him my thoughts.

"It's an idea but there's no point in going somewhere for convenience if it's not the right option. That's just a waste of time and money."

We sit staring through the tv for a while and eventually I notice the Christmas adverts are playing. I'd forgotten it was on its way.

"Anyway, there's one thing I think we should set our mind to," he says, bringing me back into the room, "I know it's going to be bitter-sweet, but I'd really like us to have a proper Christmas together for the first time. I wanted it for your mam so it would be very special to me."

I think of the small nods to Christmas he's made for my benefit over the years. The tinsel and Christmas cake were probably the only concessions.

"That would be lovely," I tell him, and I mean it. We need a new focus, and this will be perfect.

We stare at each other for the longest time, and all the while I'm reading his mind.

I know we're both thinking the very same thing. We're thinking our lives can finally start now gran's no longer with us.

I'm winded at the sudden realisation and quickly lower my eyes.

Then the guilt begins to rise to nearly choke me.

Chapter 13
Harriet Now

I really wasn't expecting an acceptance from Dolly for my invitation if I'm honest. I think Ralph may have needed to use his powers of persuasion but regardless I'm just pleased she's decided to grace us with her presence for afternoon tea.

The few times our paths have crossed, her bristles have been out, and I was at risk of a good prickling if I got too close. It can be somewhat unnerving, but I'm used to dealing with people from all walks of life so I should be used to it by now.

But this is different because this is Dolly.

"Don't take it personal," Ralph tells me, when I confess my concerns, "she'd be the same with anyone if it's any consolation."

We laugh. It is a little.

"Will you join us for moral support?" I ask him.

"You don't need me cramping your style, our Lydia will be the perfect diversion, just you wait and see."

I've joined him on the old primary school football pitch after work. It's the first meeting of the newly formed Wakeley Juniors. They're a motley crew but they're keen and Lydia's back in her element. I've paid the public liability insurance and kept schtum about it. Ralph would have worried about me being out of pocket but it's worth every penny to see the pleasure it's giving them, Ralph included.

He has them warming up, going onto fitness-building and then follows up with some practical and tactical skills. This is before they even set foot on the pitch. There are posters up around town already for the first friendly match on 15th October. It's freezing cold, but the other three boys and one girl, aged between seven and ten have been accompanied by at least one parent as per instructions in the letter sent home by the school. As Ralph told me, if we're doing it, we're doing it right. We've had a chat with the parents, and they look much the same as I did the first time that I watched Lydia play. Their expressions remind me of rabbits caught in the headlights, and they're stomping their feet to keep warm, wondering how they got here when they could be at home toasting their toes by the fireside.

Ralph and I cleared the shed between us so the team can at least have their drinks and snacks inside away from the worst of the weather. I can't help smiling to myself watching them hang onto Ralph's every word as he's pointing to his flipchart. Comical it may be, but it warms the heart.

"I'm not expecting miracles," he said, "but if they make any improvement while their enjoying themselves, that'll do for me."

Now he's watching the children with a hawk-eye. Older people are meant to be stuck in their ways, but he manages to crush the stereotype mould to do us all proud. Younger than my grandpa by twenty years or more, his boyish charm makes him appear ageless.

"I'm expecting Dolly to give me a hard time about the arrangements for the choir practice," I tell him, "I'd have done the refreshments; it was the vicar's idea to involve her."

"I had to laugh to myself when she told me. She'd never say no to the vicar, so she'll have felt cornered. It'll do her good. She might enjoy it and it's a step in the right direction with regards to Christmas. It's been a long time and perhaps some gentle changes might be just what we need. Your hearts in the right place, lass and your intentions are good. A bit of Christmas spirit wouldn't go amiss."

My eyes follow his to the team. Lydia's poised for action as shot after shot comes her way in goal. She saves some and not others but gets up ready for the next one. She'll not be beaten and swayed from her path to success.

I must take a leaf from her book I think but I'll have to tread on something even less robust than eggshells if I'm going to have a shred of hope with our Miss Dolly Hunter.

*

It's five minutes to four and Lydia and I are all set. The sandwiches, scones, and cake we made earlier are waiting under foil and the house is gleaming like a new pin. I've decided we should sit at the table as the food will be fiddly, but I really wish we could be less formal and have it from the coffee table by the fire.

I'm jittery, trying not to show it. Lydia's watching television without a care in the world. Oh, how I envy her right at this moment.

I jump up when the door knocker goes at bang on four and like some nervous tic, check my hair is in place for the hundredth time today. I open the door to Dolly standing on the second to the top step with some magazines in her hand. The simple gesture touches me, and I gush my gratitude.

"Well, I wasn't going to come empty handed, and I thought you'd have the food organised," she tells me, handing me her coat.

She's wearing one of her church ensembles; brown skirt, cream blouse and cream accessories. She dresses much older than her years, but she always looks smart, even doing her cleaning.

"Hello, Mrs Dolly," Lydia says, coming into the kitchen. She wraps her arms around Dolly's legs like she often does to greet people she knows, including Ralph. He laps it up. Dolly looks like she might faint for a second but manages to pat her head in response. Lydia's wearing a flowery dress which is similar to mine. She likes us to do this sometimes and they seemed appropriate attire for afternoon tea.

I hide a smile as I show Dolly to the table under the window. Children are the perfect icebreaker, I think. Ralph was right.

"Please take a seat. Our waitress for the afternoon is to be Miss Lydia Scott."

Dolly and Lydia smile at each other and I begin to relax just a little. I need to relax because I'll start wittering with nerves if I don't. That wouldn't be good for any of us.

Lydia brings the sandwiches over on a metal three-tier cake stand which folds out and then she sits down to join us. Sally Evans blew the dust off a pack of doilies she had in the back room, telling me there wasn't much call for them. I didn't enlighten her as to my request; I was in a rush, no time to spare for the inevitable Spanish inquisition. Dolly Hunter coming for afternoon tea was too surprising a statement to just leave hanging in the air.

"I've got one of those cake stands at home," Dolly says, "my mother had it passed down from her mother. I didn't think you could get them anymore."

"I found it in a charity shop ages ago. I prefer old things, like I was telling you. And I love a bargain."

I give her a broad smile, too broad in fact, so she looks slightly taken aback.

"I can't see there's owt wrong with that," she replies, nodding her approval, "I make a point of not paying full price for anything if I can get away with it."

I imagine money must have always been tight for Dolly. I suspect money is never far from her thoughts in one way or another. It was the same for me growing up, you don't get out of that way of thinking.

She places one of gran's lace napkins daintily on her lap as I glance at my long-stemmed glass and remember what it's there for.

"I took the liberty of getting us some fizzy wine to have with our tea if you'd like some. I wanted to do it in style."

She takes her time to carefully consider the option presented to her.

"Well as you've gone to the trouble, I'll have a glass."

As I head to the fridge Lydia starts bringing our guest up to speed about the football.

"Mr Ralph's finally got us a match sorted," she says, "I hope you'll come and watch us. I'd really like it if you did and so would mum."

Dolly smiles, no doubt coming up with a few excuses in her mind to get out of standing in the winter weather, watching ten youngsters play bad football. To be fair though, she doesn't make any … at least for the time being.

Sitting back down I pour the wine and ask Dolly if she's ever had it before. I immediately want to swallow the words back down as I can guess the answer. Nerves are most definitely getting the better of me.

"No, I haven't," she says, "I'm a gin girl, none of that fancy stuff I've seen advertised mind.

I'm glad I hadn't taken a drink yet or I'd have spit it out with surprise. Fancy Dolly being partial to a drop of the hard stuff.

"Adding a few berries and charging double is daylight robbery, but if folk get taken in by it, they've got more money than sense if you ask me."

Though I want to chuckle, I can't help but think she's spot on.

I lift my glass and say, "I'd just like to thank you for coming to join us today. I hope you'll come many more times."

I move my glass in the air to the middle of the table and Lydia clinks her glass of lemonade to mine. We wait for Dolly to realise, then she completes the circle.

Taking a sip of wine, she looks down at her plate, a little red in the face. I had to do a small toast; it wouldn't have been right otherwise but I'm glad now I didn't go overboard.

"I hear you're forming a choir," she says.

Dolly doesn't let the grass grow and gets straight down to business. Here we go I think, I must be careful not to trip over my words.

"Yes, well, there's only seven of us at the moment, so it will be a low-key choir by the look of it."

A strange little laugh escapes me.

"I heard the vicar asked you to do the refreshments. I didn't expect him to as I planned on doing them myself. I'll speak to him if you'd like me to."

She puts her sandwich down, a look of horror on her face.

"No, I've told him I'll do it and I will. There's no need for that."

"Oh, well, I'll bring the refreshments along and give you a hand then, so you don't have to go to too much trouble."

Her face softens slightly.

"Right you are, then. I'm sure we'll manage to give nine people a cup of tea and a biscuit between us."

She busies herself choosing her next sandwich.

"Have you always lived in the same house?" Lydia asks now.

Dolly eyes glaze as though she's casting her mind back.

"We moved to this row after my father had a promotion. They're the best two rows in town as the view of the woods opposite means they're very sought after," she pauses, "well, they were once."

I can picture Dolly and her parents being so excited about moving to this row, my gran and grandpa will have been the same. She's proud of her little house still, and so she should be. It's like a diamond twinkling amongst a stack of coal.

"I really like it here," Lydia tells her, "And l especially like it that you and Mr Ralph live so close by."

"Thank you," Dolly says, the corners of her mouth tilting slightly.

How proud I am of my charming little daughter.

"I was thinking," Lydia goes on, "please would you let me play with your hair and do your makeup like mum does sometimes. I get bored just playing with Daisy all the time."

Oh, I wasn't expecting her to ask that. Dolly gulps a mouthful of wine noisily then coughs once and then again. I rush to help her out of her discomfort.

"Miss Dolly does her own hair and doesn't seem to need very much makeup, so you'll have to make do with me."

"I think she'd look lovely if I did her. You do mum and you say I'm the best."

I shrug my shoulders at Dolly and raise my eyes, lost for words. She gives me a tight smile.

"Well, I suppose it wouldn't do any harm. I do need to set my hair tonight for church tomorrow anyway, so I'll let you have a comb of it. I can always wash the makeup off if I don't like it."

Lydia's face drops.

"I'm sure I will like it, mind," she says quickly.

I think the wine must have gone to her head.

We decamp to the front room, and I take the bottle of wine from the fridge to bring with us.

"Where would you like me to sit?" Dolly asks Lydia.

If you sit in the chair by the fire, I'll get my special brushes and makeup from upstairs."

Dolly does as she's bid, settling herself in the chair where Ralph usually sits.

"I'm going to have another glass as it's a special occasion if you'd care to join me," I say.

She gives it some thought for a second or two.

"Why not? Just half a glass for me though please," she says.

I was expecting a refusal. The poor woman is so far out of her comfort zone, I think as Lydia appears with her bag of tricks. She puts a towel around Dolly's shoulders like she's at the hairdressers and lays her tools out neatly on the coffee table.

Then she spends the next half an hour working her magic, not only with the makeover but also with the conversation.

I discover so much about the Dolly of old: How her mum liked to curl her hair with heated rollers every morning, how she coloured it blonde until the day she died. How there used to be a hairdresser in Wakeley, but it closed years ago so she's always done it herself since. How she doesn't like to wear too much makeup on her face generally, because it makes her feel like she needs a good wash.

Lydia is listening as intently as I am. The wine was a good idea, I think as I soak up every detail of the picture that she's painting for us. I've waited a long time for even a snippet of information from Dolly herself.

"My best friend lived in this house you know, before she…moved away," Dolly says, "now you'd have liked doing her hair. It was as black as the night and the shiniest

I've ever seen then and since. I used to tell her how much I wanted hair like hers."

I catch my breath at the description and wait for more but she goes silent.

"How're you getting on?" she asks Lydia eventually. She's been deep in concentration and quiet for once.

Placing her brush back down on the coffee table, Lydia stands back to check if her work is complete. She smooths a little smudge of powder on the end of Dolly's nose. Dolly twitches it twice, to make her giggle. Satisfied now with the results Lydia holds up my hand mirror for Dolly to take a good look at herself.

There's no mistaking how attractive she is if you bother to look carefully but she can mislead you. Her manner can make her appear stiff and old before her time. She's both, but she's still got plenty going for her. The set curls have been loosened by Lydia into soft waves, the many tones of grey now catching the light. I've noticed this before. Although she's only a novice, Lydia's had plenty of practice and the overall transformation is remarkable. Dolly clearly appreciates the reflection staring back at her in the same way we do. She turns her head this way and that, admiring herself.

"What do you think?" Lydia asks.

Dolly moves her face closer to the mirror. Raising her eyebrows, she turns down her mouth, nodding slowly.

"I agree with your mum," she says, "you really are the best in town."

Lydia's smile lights up her face and we both smile back at her. What a difference a smile makes, Dolly is almost glowing.

I've seen more than a little of what mum must have seen in Dolly this afternoon. I understand now why she was so fond of her. Little does she know, but this simple little gathering has been a long-held dream come true for me.

We sit chatting about football for a while longer until Dolly stands up to go. I tell her we'll walk her home as it's dark.

"I can walk the ten steps by myself, thank you all the same," she tells me, briskly.

After some persuasion, she reluctantly agrees we can watch her from the gate, reminding us she's looked after herself for many a year.

I think then about how the people of the town are living hand to mouth, yet crime is non-existent. I know this from the statistics at the town hall. Dolly lives in blissful ignorance of the dangers the majority of the world faces each day. I envy her such peace of mind and sense of security.

"Thanks for a very pleasant afternoon," she says, putting her coat on, "I'll see you both in the morning."

"So, will you come and watch me play football, Mrs Dolly?" Lydia asks, her round brown eyes like a puppy dog staring up at her.

What excuse will Dolly give I wonder.

She takes a breath.

"Well, if it means so much to you, I will."

Surely, I've misheard for the second time today. Lydia wraps her arms around Dolly's legs again, but this time she's not quite so taken aback. She pats the curly springs of Lydia's ponytail.

When I open the back door Ralph is on his way to the rubbish bin, binbag in hand.

He looks then looks again at the new Dolly. Then when Lydia tells him that she's coming to watch the match, his mouth opens slightly.

"Well, you'd better shut your cake hole as a train's coming, Ralph Kellett," Dolly says, with a hint of a smile. Her cheeks are flushed from the fire and drinking wine in the afternoon. She sounds like a teenager. I can imagine her saying exactly those words to him all those years ago.

My mind goes straight to mum.

As Ralph grins and shakes his head at Dolly and we say our goodbyes, I can't help my thoughts going back to the pair of them. I watch Dolly go up the snowy ginnel and into her back gate like she's done since she was a small child. She waves before she disappears out of sight.

Why can't Ralph bring himself to tell her how he feels about her I wonder as I walk with Lydia back into the warmth of our cosy little house. Why won't he tell her he couldn't marry Ruth and returned to Wakeley because of her all those years ago?

I know the answer well enough. Sometimes you go down a certain path so far you can't turn back, or if you're walking the path with someone else, you run the risk of having to turn back without them.

So apparently, that makes two of us. Two secret admirers who are hesitant to profess undying love to Dolly Hunter.

However, with her armour intact and her sword always at the ready to draw to protect herself, I doubt anybody would blame us.

Chapter 14
Harriet Then

I've given the entire house a good bottoming as gran used to call it years ago, cleaning every nook and cranny so it sparkles as it should this time of year.

She didn't wake up one day in the terribly depressed state of mind she had at the end. It was a long time happening, showing itself in subtle ways. Until I was older, you wouldn't have exactly called her happy by any means, but she was functioning, getting by. I think now that was the key; subconsciously, she was waiting for me to be able to fend for myself more. I could feel her love for me though right to the end.

It's still daylight but I put the light on in the front room to admire my efforts. Grandpa will be on his way back soon with the last bits and pieces we need for tomorrow. We've had the bitter-sweet December we expected, but we made sure it erred more on the sweet side. This is something he's always wanted for me and my mum before; to have a Christmas, but even more, to feel a Christmas.

A nine-foot tree was delivered the second week of December. As I look at it now, it stands about a foot from the ceiling to make room for the copper star which sits atop. The white lights are ready and waiting to be switched on as dusk falls. Of all the pleasures to be had this time of year, the tree has been my pinnacle. The day itself hasn't arrived yet, but I know already what I've been missing.

November was spent buying decorations and food, some I'd never seen before: hazelnuts, dates, sugared fruits. We made a garland of eucalyptus strung with dried oranges, cinnamon sticks, and pinecones, and draped it over the high mantle. It spills down over the side and the fairy lights twinkle amongst the foliage. We went along to the Christmas market at the town hall and bought some new and some vintage glass baubles for the tree. The old Wessel cups are my favourite though: grandpa had saved them all these years from his childhood. They're rich in colour and catch the light best of all. I think of them hanging on the tree when grandpa was a boy. The thought warms me.

When you walk in the house from the cold, a mix of wonderful scents greet you. The smell of the fresh tree, the garland, the Christmas pudding, and brandy-soaked cake seem to fill every room. I can't help thinking about gran and how she missed out on these simple pleasures all her life. But then you can't miss something you never had.

This time of year, I often imagine the house in days gone by. I picture the staff, busy downstairs in the cellar kitchen, bustling about with festive purpose. I think of the family in grand clothes, someone playing the piano we inherited to accompany the carol singing. I can imagine them exchanging gifts around the tree, the fireplace glowing with Christmas cosiness. I'm glad the house has retained so much of its history, and we recognised and cherished it. Most of the row was bought for pennies in the sixties when people were excited by the thought of a newly built home to move into. It's worth a pretty penny now because of its grandeur, but most of all because of its prime position on the outskirts of the city.

"Well, whatever we haven't got, we'll have to do without now," grandpa says, bringing the coldness inside with him through the back door. He puts his slippers on straight away so as not to spoil the gleaming tiles and all my hard work.

"We've enough to feed an army, never mind the two of us," I laugh, helping him with the many bags filled with Christmas treats.

He looks around the kitchen.

"By, you have been busy, it's fair twinkling in here," he tells me.

"Wait until you see the front room after tea," I say proudly, "no peeking before mind."

I put the stand pie, as he calls it and all the cheeses and chutneys in the fridge. There's fresh ham from the bone, fresh stuffing for tomorrow too and he tells me he's left the turkey and vegetables in a cool bag in the shed as we'll be doing them first thing in the morning. It's just as well because there's no room at the inn indoors.

We're having the ham with fresh bread and butter and tinned fruit and cream to finish. It was the tea he used to have on Christmas Eve when he was growing up. He's recreating the rituals one by one, and I can tell he's revelling in the nostalgia of it all.

"My mother, your great grandmother, used to say we should eat well but plain and simple fare on the day before the feast."

How he must have loved my dear gran to give up these pleasures. I can see already how difficult it would be to forgo.

After tea we head down the long passageway towards the front room. I ask him to wait outside a minute, shutting the door behind me. I place the university brochures I was looking at earlier in the rack, throw some more coal on the fire and stoke the flames. Finally, I switch on the fairy lights and turn off the lamps before drawing the curtains. The scene is now set.

"You can come in now, grandpa," I call.

He pokes his head round the door and his mouth drops. I grin at him.

We stand side by side looking around the room in awe. Between us we've done a fine job and it's lovely to appreciate the result of all our hard work these last weeks. I know he's thinking about gran because I am. I close my eyes to the sharp pain and think how to change the mood.

"Come on, first one to sit down picks the film we watch tomorrow," I say quickly.

In typical fashion, he pretends to rush to the chair, but I know he's going to let me win.

"Oh, I nearly forgot, I found an old Christmas record in town earlier this month. I put it by for us to play today.

He heads to our old record player and carefully places the vinyl on the turntable. The familiar crackle sounds before Nat King Cole begins to sing *Merry Christmas to You*. Now this one I know, like many other Christmas songs from the department stores playing them over the years.

We sit opposite each other soaking up the fruits of our labour with the wonderful music playing low in the background. Grandpa indulges in a couple of whiskies, and he fixes me a custard yellow drink he calls 'Christmas in a glass', but the real name is a 'snowball'. It's peaceful listening to the music and as the night draws on, he has a couple more drinks. He's chattier than I've ever known him as he never drank alcohol in the house when gran was alive.

He's telling me all about his childhood Christmases, in full flow. It's not about the gifts, he says, it's about the feeling it gives you inside, the warm glow.

He becomes a little subdued and I imagine he's thinking about gran. He stares into his glass in a world of his own. I'm not sure what to do.

"Are you alright, grandpa?" I ask quietly.

Sighing, he put his glass on the side table.

"Just ignore me, love, I'm being a maudlin old beggar. I've had one too many whiskies, but I didn't want to spoil tonight. I wanted it to be perfect and live up to your expectations."

"You'll not spoil it. If it's bothering you, you should tell me, we've always told each other our worries. Anyway, we've still got tomorrow."

I give him a small smile of encouragement.

"I suppose you're right," he says, "I've just keep thinking about that Christmas we had in Wakeley way back. I think about it often, but it's become a bit of a monster tonight, probably because my feelings are heightened … and that," he nods towards his whisky glass, "I can't shake the memory now."

Little does he know I'm all ears, having wanted to know more about what happened when my mother was a child for so long. I couldn't raise it with him as I wouldn't want to open old wounds.

"Yes, I've heard mention of the accident in a couple of mum's letters from Dolly," I say.

He stares at the tree, reliving a time I imagine when he lived another life in another place long before I was even thought about.

"It might be the Christmas tree which is bringing back all the memories. Dolly and her mam and dad loved to put theirs up early, way before everybody else and it gave me a glow to see it as I went to and from work in the darkness of December. It's Dolly who sticks in my mind the most, more than her mother if truth be told. She was such a good friend to your mam throughout her life and she stepped up when she became ill, waiting for her heart operation. Every day she came to visit her, every single day. She was only a young lass herself and she should have been out having a good time, but she said she wasn't missing a thing. They had an affinity few are lucky enough to find."

He swallows and I don't like the look on his face.

"It must have been in the genes because I found the same affinity with her dad. Eric was my best friend, my only friend. Everyone else I considered to be colleagues or acquaintances. Looking back, I just didn't need anyone else, he was all I really needed.

Joan, Dolly's mam, and your gran were friendly enough but not like we were. I think of Eric still like a brother. Our mothers brought us up like brothers, we were together all the time. I had a sister, as you know who you sadly never met, but he was the brother I never had. We loved to get into each other's ribs, loved the banter, but we never had what I'd call a cross word. It wasn't that we tried not to, we just didn't. Even when I was made foreman, he was chuffed for me, not jealous like some were. I'd have felt the same for him; his achievements were mine and mine were his."

I can see the fire as a tiny image flickering in grandpa's eyes, I'm watching him so intently. I've been patiently waiting four years since I was thirteen and given Dolly's letters to hear this tale.

"Eric and Joan would have liked more children after Dolly, but it never happened. Your gran and I decided to pour all our time, money, and energy into your mother with her being so unwell from being born. She was a rare gem. You remind me of her, a chip off the old diamond as your gran and I used to call you.

I started working as an apprentice at *Worthies* at the same time as Eric. If you lived in Wakeley in those days, you knew where you'd end up. You didn't question it or feel lucky, it was just how it was. But we *were* lucky.

Friday nights would see us down the club, Saturdays the girls would join us, well, before your mother became too ill. We had a good sound roof over our heads, plenty of food, warm fires, and a job for life. Times were simple but solid, satisfying. We didn't want for owt, not a thing.

When I was made foreman, I didn't like it at first. It didn't sit right with me, and I was a bit soft to start with. I realised with experience however there's a way to oversee people and you don't have to lord it over them. Mostly, I needed the extra money and I think that was the reason I was chosen over the other lads.

It's hard to believe now, but the biggest battle I had on my hands as foreman was smoking. Just about everyone smoked in those days, at home, in the club, and at work.

It was just a part of our lives like eating your dinner, but we weren't completely ignorant. We knew about the dangers of smoking in the copperworks as there was so much around which would go up in flames.

Most of the men had a quick cigarette when they went for a toilet break: a whole shift was a long time to go without a drag. So, the rule was that we ran the tab end under the tap before we binned it, on the off chance we might not put it out properly if we were rushing back to work. I had to play the game and remind the blokes every so often, but it was as commonplace as breathing."

He takes a long breath then rubs the back of his neck. I want him to stop but then I don't because I'm waiting to discover what happened. He closes his eyes briefly before going on.

"So, you can imagine how shocked, no horrified, we were to get through the doors after dinner one day, laughing and bantering and then not being able to see past the end of our noses for smoke. Acrid, lung-clawing smoke. The silence filtered from the front to the back of the line like wildfire but then all hell broke loose in a matter of seconds. Men were running everywhere. I smashed the fire alarm with the little hammer always hanging at the side, never thinking I'd ever have to use it, and the bell rang around the building. The deafening sound still does a fair job at haunting me even now.

A few men had the good sense to turn and run straight back downstairs, but many of us had the idea we could contain it. It's that old 'fight or flight' thing. The fire had already got a good hold and was swallowing the building, coming closer by the second and I realise of course now a few buckets of water weren't going to help. Thomas Worthington appeared, shouting for everybody to get out and I realised too late that the stairway we'd come up was getting blocked by fire. We were coughing by then, and I was ushering everyone to the back stairs. Ironically, it was the fire exit. In the seventies, health and safety wasn't at the top of the agenda like today. The fire door was always wide open, and we never questioned it. In my mind I knew if I could get everyone to go down the back stairs before the fire spread in that direction, I could shut the door and it would give them time to get out. Bear in mind, there were hundreds of us. It all seemed so straightforward, but mass panic can make the easiest task impossible.

I kept shouting over and over again, "Get to the back stairs, lads, get to the back stairs!" and eventually, like sheep they all followed me. It wasn't calm and orderly, there were people jostling, coughing, spluttering, falling but I stood at the top waiting for them to get through as organised as I could. After what seemed like a lifetime, there was nobody else to be seen. I could see down the corridor that the fire had engulfed the second floor and encroaching, and I started to pull the door. The hinges were rusted stuck so I went around the other side to push it and managed to get it just short of halfway. I was panicking myself, pulling with all the strength I could muster, and Thomas Worthington was pulling me from behind and another man pulling him, and so on in a human chain. That blasted door was going nowhere.

I admit it, I wanted us all to flee down the stairs, but it was too risky. The chain disbanded and I could see some men further down the stairway waiting for me to come and join them. Thomas and I kept tugging with all our strength, the heat starting to hurt it was getting so close. We were flagging, I for one wanted to give up but something was stopping me. Finally, I gave it one last heave. The door slammed with such force towards me it knocked me off my feet and then Thomas, like a couple of dominoes. I didn't have time to be relieved, but I got to my feet thinking how I'd read superhuman strength was to be found in a crisis.

Running down the stairs at the back of the line, your gran and your mother's face were at the front of my mind. I wanted to see them like an ache, and I remember thinking your gran would never cope alone without me.

Outside the fire brigade had just arrived and I realised then how short a time had elapsed. It seemed like I'd lived an eternity in about ten short minutes. More fire engines and ambulances arrived, and some men were taken to hospital with smoke inhalation. People were scuttling about all over the place; c'workers, wives, mothers, small babies, and children. I was looking for your gran and I found her, she ran to me, and I held her to me like a man clinging to a life raft. I was worried about your mother on her own, but she told me a neighbour was with her. You remember the one I've told you about before, Mrs Turrell.

I tucked your gran under my arm to weave around and find Eric. I asked around but nobody had seen him. I didn't think much of it at first; it was like trying to find a needle in a haystack.

Eventually, I saw Thomas Worthington beckoning me over. By then, we'd found Dolly's mother and we were all as frustrated and non-plussed as each other, thinking Eric would turn up any minute.

Except he never did.

Dolly's mother fell into my arms when Thomas told her what had happened. I caught her but my knees were buckling under the shock too. I couldn't take it in. None of us could.

It turned out Eric was my superhuman strength. Eric, being Eric had been up on the third floor and made sure everyone up there was out before trying to escape himself.

Eric was the one who saved us all. He reached the third floor landing and could see us struggling with the door so he took it upon himself to push the door from the other side.

Grandad pauses, and stares into a painful past only his mind's eye can see, his rheumy eyes glistening.

"He more than likely knew he wouldn't get out himself as the fire was right on his heels.

We took it in alright when the stretcher came past with Eric under the blanket. Poor, poor Joan, I'll never get the distressing scene out of my mind. Never."

He runs his hand through his hair, his taut face ashen at the memory.

"The worst of it all was that Eric had to wait a long time to become the hero he is now in everyone's eyes. A man called Brian Addlebury had started a rumour that Eric was the one smoking in the toilets. The one who was responsible for all the devastation and further potential loss of life. Back then, Brian was a pillar of the community. We had no reason to think he was lying. That bloody no-mark, excuse my language, went on with his lying to become Dolly's stepfather."

I've read about some of this in Dolly's letters. My one wish for so long has been to piece all the fragments of information together. Now, my curiosity is satisfied only to be replaced by an incredible sadness for Dolly, for Joan, for grandpa … for the whole town.

"Anyway, that's a whole other story. We'd known Brian all our lives; went to school with him, worked with him, drank down the club with him, picked him up after his wife Doreen supposedly died, tipped up for Ruth, but it turned out we didn't know him at all. Evil b…"

He remembers himself just in time, shaking his head.

"I still missed Eric like a crippling pain, despite thinking for long enough he was the cause of the fire. It could have been any of us, it just so happened it was Eric I thought then. I was secretly glad to leave Wakeley and get away from the terrible cloud which hung over the town. If your mother hadn't been sick, I would have stayed, and who knows what would have become of me. The pain cloyed at me, followed me everywhere; I just couldn't be rid of it. The finality of the situation was the worst pain to carry, of simply knowing I would never see Eric again."

My heart is heavy, and I have a terrible crushing pain in my chest. I can relate to that feeling now I think, because of gran. The incredulity of it all is galling.

"It was years before the truth came out that Brian was the culprit. He'd chucked his cigarette out of the toilet window because he couldn't be bothered to wait his turn at the sink. The accident report said the fire had started in a pile of wood off cuts and rubbish the works' chippies had left next to the toilet block.

To blame a dead man who couldn't defend himself is the lowest of the low in my book, in anyone's. Young

Ralph Kellett who worked with us, collared me on my way home from work one day after finding out the truth from Brian's daughter.

Ralph was due to marry her, but he couldn't go through with it for all sorts of reasons. He was in a right state because Dolly's mother had married Brian by then and if Ralph told anyone it would upset the applecart for both her and Dolly. Ralph thought they were playing happy families and I didn't know any better as I was living here.

Ralph didn't want me to tell your mother because he knew she and Dolly kept in touch, so I found him some lodgings in Thorndale. The soft lad ended up marrying his landlady within two minutes of him landing on her doorstep, but he went back to Wakeley as soon as he found out about Brian's true colours being revealed, and Dolly's mother sending him packing. I'd have liked to have been a fly on the wall that day.

I was left with the guilt: guilt for surviving the fire; for leaving a sinking ship of a town even though I had good reason; for living in such a lovely house; for having such a good job; but most of all for believing Brian Addlebury's lie."

Lowering his head grandpa puts his hand up to wipe his eyes. I've never seen him cry before. I panic, unsure what to do as tears sting my eyes.

"It sounds like he was a master of deceit," I say, quickly through my tight throat, "you shouldn't blame yourself. It looks like he had everyone fooled."

My words make him sit up straight in his chair and smile. Not a very convincing smile, but it's not long before my old grandpa is making his way back to me and I can start to breathe properly again.

"I should have left the top on that whisky bottle," he says with a nod towards it.

I'm only too glad to have him back after reliving his traumatic tale with him.

"It seems to me like you needed to get it off your chest. I think you'll be glad you did when you have chance to think about it."

"You might be right. So, now you know the story which has haunted me for half my life. But you can't alter the past Hattie, you can only learn from it. We've had more than our fair share of upset but in and amongst it all we've still been lucky for many reasons."

"I'm glad you told me," I say quietly, and despite the sadness, I am. "Have you seen Dolly since you left?"

"I wrote to tell her about your mother. It was a difficult letter to write but she had to find out from us, and your gran was in no fit state. I'm not sure what good it would do for either of us if we met each other. It's not easy to open old wounds as you can see," he points to his glass, "it took nigh on half a bottle of whisky to get me to open up about this."

He quickly claps his hands together I suspect to bring himself back to the present. He brings himself back into this room by the fireside, by the tree with me in the midst of his longed-awaited Christmastime.

"Right, enough of all this self-indulgence, lets plan what we're going to do tomorrow. It'll be the best Christmas ever, love, just you wait and see."

He was right. It was a truly wonderful Christmas, better than I could ever have imagined. The feeling it gave me was enough to keep me warm all year, and it was made even more special by the small locket grandpa presented to me. Two tiny photographs of mum and dad were side by side within it.

And when I got into bed on Christmas Day night, I'd made a promise to myself. I'd been thinking about Dolly Hunter for long enough, I carried her around with me in my head. So, I made a promise that night, one I was prepared to go more than the extra mile to keep: Come what may, and however long it took me, I was going to thank Dolly for all she'd done. More than that, I was going to work out some way to repay her on behalf of mum, gran, grandpa but, most of all, on behalf of myself.

I knew by then though that actions speak far louder than words. I needed to work on a solid, unstoppable, copper-bottomed plan.

True to my word, even while I was studying for six years to be a solicitor, even when I met and married Daniel, even after I had Lydia, I was still working steadily on that plan.

Every detail was being carefully mapped out. Slow and steady wins the race was my mantra, I wasn't going to let myself down by leaving anything to chance.

I have many vivid memories of that Christmas. In the end the sweetness of it far outweighed the bitterness. But the main memory which sticks in my mind was the least dramatic yet most profound, as is so often the case.

I remember it as being the one where grandpa screwed the top back on the whisky bottle for the very last time.

Chapter 15
Harriet Now

"All I'm saying is, give it time. You've only played four matches, you need to be patient," Dolly says.

"I just want us to win one match, that's all, you don't understand how important it would be to us," Lydia sighs, piling biscuits on a plate.

The shadow of a smile appears on Dolly's lips, and she looks away, no doubt amused at the dramatic outburst.

Nine of us make up the choir now. The only criteria to join was to love singing. We're practicing carols with me accompanying them on the piano. I dug out my old music and after a vote we decided on three carols. It's slow going, especially with the harmony for '*O Holy Night*', but there's still a few weeks left. In any case, we're enjoying ourselves and filling the church with music.

"I'm beginning to understand," Dolly says, rattling the lid back on the huge tea urn. It hadn't seen the light of day for many a year.

Their conversation makes me think of the first time I saw Dolly in her raincoat and lace-up shoes walking over the playing field to stand with the rest of the turnout watching the match. Her handbag was hanging over her arm, and she was clutching the top of her hood to stop it blowing off.

The scene may have been comical, like Ralph and his flipchart, but I was touched. I'm still touched she's prepared to stand in the cold and often snow a couple of hours a week. Football appears to have become common ground. Ralph goes round to Dolly's with Lydia most afternoons and I doubt there'll be much else on the conversation agenda.

"I see Dolly's dressed for the weather," Ralph laughed, when he spotted her that day, "but then I don't suppose she's had much call for football togs before."

Ralph's still taking his coaching responsibilities very seriously. He arranged for one of the dads from Thorndale Primary to referee and persuaded Sally Evans to buy a few bibs in return for a mention in the school newsletter. There's a bigger turnout each week from Wakeley and even from Thorndale as word spread. Dolly's engaging more and more with the football and with the people.

But then everybody knows Dolly.

I watch the choir drift in one by one or in pairs. I've always been in a choir of some description since primary school, and it seemed natural I tried to form one in Wakeley. I was particularly pleased when three men turned up to join. The choir is causing quite a stir in town and there's more people coming along to church on a Sunday, much to the vicar's delight. This is a beautiful church which needs to be revered. Sometimes you don't appreciate the value of something when it's always been quietly sitting there under your nose. I can see the wonder of the building through fresh eyes.

"Evening, everyone," I say, when the choir are settled in their seats, "thanks as ever for turning up on this freezing cold night. I know it's never much warmer in here."

The church is an ornate freezer box and a couple of electric fan heaters don't make much difference to the temperature.

"Time's speeding along to the concert so I think we might need to meet a couple of times a week in the run up if possible. Let's start by doing our usual warm up scales."

We're never going to win any awards, extra practice or not, but the piano and acoustics help. Anyway, much like the football, it's all about the focus and sense of community. They're always the crucial ingredients.

At the end of the hour, Dolly and Lydia leave their seats to organise the refreshments. They work in a cramped little makeshift kitchen area I set up around the back of the church, but it does the job.

"I can't remember when we last had a choir, can you, Dolly?" Joyce Pinner asks, taking a cup of tea from the row provided.

"I was at school," Dolly says, "so a very long time ago, over fifty years anyway."

"Fifty years!" Lydia exclaims, her eyes widening, "You're never as old as that, Mrs Dolly, are you?"

Lydia picks up another biscuit and I whisper to her the remark was a little rude.

"Sorry," she says to Dolly with a solemn expression, "I didn't know it was rude to tell somebody if they're old."

Dolly smiles down at her, unfazed while the choir stifle their laughs, not entirely sure like me what's really going through Dolly's mind.

I notice her hair is a little softer nowadays, more combed out since her makeover. I've even spotted face cream and a touch of colour on her cheeks to accompany her lipstick. I suspect Lydia's had a hand in it.

"I for one, am enjoying coming," Joyce says, placing her cup back on her saucer. Tea must always be served in a cup and saucer for Dolly.

They all nod and murmur in agreement and I can't deny how nice it is to hear it.

Joyce suddenly turns her full attention on me.

"There seems to be plenty of activity at the town hall these days, Harriet," she says, "Bernie must be keeping you busy. Don't be overdoing it mind, he's a lazy old devil."

I feel Dolly's eyes on me along with everyone else's and immediately tense.

"We work quite well together, and he lets me go at my own pace which is good," I say.

I take a sip of tea to disguise my discomfort.

"I don't see much action. What's he got you doing?" Dolly asks, her face never leaving mine.

Darn Joyce Pinner I think, this was not a conversation I was expecting to be having. I didn't know she had a front row seat to the townhall from where she lives.

"Erm, well there's talk of a few more jobs at *Lumley's*," I say.

It appears I'm backed into a corner with no way out.

"Really? How many?" Joyce asks.

I hesitate so they start speculating. This is big news, but I didn't want to be sharing it just yet.

"Oh, you know, it's early days and nothing's been finalised. I'd appreciate you keeping it to yourselves just in case it doesn't work out."

Of course, we will they tell me, of course. Dolly is still looking at me.

I'm now looking at the hallowed ground of the church floor, willing it to swallow me up whole.

*

Somehow this year it feels premature for once.

The last day of November is always the start of the Christmas seasons I've come to know and love. It's all Lydia's known but it definitely feels too early this year.

So, I try to shake it off by thinking of grandpa saying to me in times of doubt, "Be you, be true, and you'll know what to do."

With this in mind, I decide to do what I always do and take Lydia into town to buy a chocolate advent calendar and the tree.

"I'm going to wear a skirt with the red top I've been saving today," she says, "what are you going to wear, mum?"

I consider my options for a second.

"I think my cream woollen dress will be appropriate for the occasion."

She smiles as she heads into the bathroom, her face full of excitement for the day ahead.

I lay back in bed and think about how mum must have done the same. I chose this room as it was hers and I can sense her all around me. It's quiet at the back of the house and Lydia loves having the grand front bedroom all to herself. She tells me she likes looking at the tops of the trees in the woodland over the road when she wakes up, it makes her feel like she's in the countryside.

I wish mum could have felt the excitement of advent in her day, like we are today. The build-up is most certainly the best part for me.

I've been deliberating for some time about making the trip to Thorndale, so I haven't asked Ralph if he'd like to join us. We knock on his door mid-morning to ask the question. It's last minute but he'll have been up hours, doing his jobs then reading the paper.

Opening the door with his soapy clean face and shiny white hair, he's the picture of vitality. He looks ten years younger than when we arrived, a walking advertisement for what a sense of purpose can do for you.

Ralph's eyes flick between the two of us then he tells us to step in out of the cold.

"We're going to start Christmas today and go into town for my calendar and a tree. Will you come with us?" Lydia gushes at him.

"By, you two are early birds," he says, looking a little taken aback. I'm unsure whether he's referring to the request to join us or the premature start to our festivities.

He hesitates so I think he's going to turn down our invitation for a moment but then he sees Lydia waiting expectantly for an answer.

He smiles suddenly and I enjoy the relief flowing through me.

"Well, it looks as though I've been made me an offer I can't refuse. What fool would want to miss out on the company of two lovely young ladies?" he asks, grabbing his keys and wallet.

"Do you think Mrs Dolly would like to come with us?" Lydia asks.

Ralph and I glance at each other as he's buttoning his Sunday best overcoat, as he calls it for our trip to town. I can see he's considering his answer carefully.

"She's still at the vicarage," he says, no doubt thinking as I am that Dolly wouldn't take so kindly to being thrown an impromptu invitation to go shopping. She'd drop it like hot potato and back away.

"Oh right, well it will be a nice surprise for her to see our tree then."

"It will that, it will that," he says, taking Lydia's hand as we walk around the front of the row to the van. I've only used it a few times and it's a nightmare to park, but it means we can buy a bigger tree.

"I'll treat us to a bit of dinner at Polly's," Ralph says.

"This is going to be the best day ever," Lydia tells us, and Ralph and I share a laugh.

"Oh, to be seven again," Ralph whispers, "Christmas handed to you on a plate to stuff yourself to the ginnels."

He realises too late what he's said but I pat his arm and shake my head, telling him I'm making up for lost time.

Two hours later, we've been to Bakers, the one and only department store in Thorndale, and Lydia's chosen her chocolate advent calendar with a dancing snowman. We bought an extra one for Ralph, who looked like a big kid when we handed it to him, and one for Dolly. I'm not sure what she'll make of it, but we couldn't leave her out.

Lydia's chosen a tiny glass reindeer to add to her collection of special baubles. The tree we bought from the grocer who's diversifying for the Christmas period, is tucked safely in the back of the van. Not surprisingly we were first in the queue, so we got the best of the bunch.

We're waiting for our jam roly-poly and custard for pudding in *Polly's*. It's one of the many school-dinner type puddings that grandpa talks about, and we replicate from time to time. We've spoken every day on the phone, and we do a videocall once a week.

I still miss him.

Good Honest Grub is the strapline of *Polly's*, and you simply can't beat it, especially on a cold wintry day like this.

"Will you help us put the tree up when we get home?" Lydia asks Ralph.

167

"I'd be honoured, Miss Lydia," he tells her, inclining his head.

She giggles, saying then, "Maybe we can help you put yours up tomorrow."

Ralph looks awkward, resolutely avoiding eye contact.

"I don't usually bother with a tree, but I'd love to come and see yours as many times as you'll let me."

Lydia's mouth drops. If I'm honest she's mirroring how I feel but I'm more adept at hiding my emotions.

"You've got to have a tree!" Lydia tells Ralph, "Your house will look so sad at Christmas without one."

He wipes his mouth on his napkin, sitting back in his chair to consider his thoughts on the subject.

"Do you know what, you're right," he says after a moment, "I don't know what I've been thinking all these years. Shall we go back to Barkers and get a tree and some baubles? I think a tree which I can bring out every year will be better for me.

She smiles and nods once, content now the universe has shifted back into alignment.

"You'll need some fairy lights too. You've got to have fairy lights they're the best bit."

"Well, we better get cracking then," he says, getting up to pay the bill as we thank him for treating us to lunch.

As we all clamber out of the van at home, I spot Dolly going up the path to her house. I wave and I'm reminded of the first day we arrived. This time she waves back and smiles. We've come a long way in a couple of months, I think, by Dolly standards at least. Thank goodness for the wonder of children. I know now I wouldn't have been able to make an inroad so quickly with Dolly if it wasn't for Lydia.

It's half past one already and we've still got plenty to do. Ralph takes our tree inside then goes next door to drop his, while I put the kettle on. Lydia's brought our baubles and lights from upstairs and placed her advent calendar on the dresser by the time he returns.

Once Ralph has positioned the tree by the window and placed it safely in its stand, I wrap the lights around, switching them on and squinting to check they're in the perfect position. Satisfied, we start carefully unwrapping the baubles together.

"You've got some pretty ones, mind," Ralph says.

I've been collecting them since the first Christmas with grandpa after gran died and I've bought Lydia a special one every year since she was born.

Lydia's chatting away, but I notice Ralph is a little quiet for once. I want to ask if he's alright, but I know he wouldn't say either way in front of Lydia.

We switch the lights back on when we've finished arranging the baubles. Standing back to admire the results of our joint efforts, we agree we've done a fine job between us. It's a beautiful sight in the early dusk of the winter afternoon.

"You picked a good shape," Ralph tells me, "It looks bonny, Hattie."

I smile at him, proud of his approval.

"Can we put your tree up now and then look at them both in the window from over the road?" Lydia asks, still staring at the tree.

Ralph's expression darkens, and my heart falls. He's not himself today at all.

"If you don't mind, I've had enough excitement for one day, Miss Lydia," he tells her, "And it feels a bit early for me to start Christmas at my house, but you can help me another day if you would."

I step in quickly before she has chance to speak and make Ralph feel worse than he clearly does already.

"The best thing about Christmas is something called anticipation," I tell her, "It means if you do everything at once you have nothing to look forward to. The build-up is the most special part."

"Alright," she says, not entirely convinced, "we can still have a look at ours outside can't we, and then we can take the advent calendar up to Mrs Dolly?"

"Deal," I say, but Ralph still seems to be all at sixes and sevens and doesn't look my way. He joins us in pulling our coats and boots on before we head down the front path.

We stand at the end of the gate to take in the scene. In the fading light the tree shimmers against the darkening sky and the black stone houses below it. I'm reminded of the contrast of the high-rise flats and the parkland on my thirteenth birthday, a lump appearing in my throat at the memory. This is a day to add to my collection.

"I've never seen a more beautiful sight," Ralph says, "not for a long, long time."

"See," Lydia says, "I bet you're glad you got your tree now."

I'm glad to be able to laugh along with Ralph at her indignant tone. She flies up the path to grab the advent calendar for Dolly and tucks it under her arm on her way back. I never lock the door if I nip out, I realise. I must feel safe living in Wakeley.

"I'll leave you to it," Ralph says, but I'll see you for practice tomorrow," he shouts after Lydia.

He makes a hasty retreat even before Lydia gets chance to give him her usual leg hug. She looks as bemused as I feel but he's waving us off and disappearing out of sight before she can quiz him further. I admit I was expecting him to join us.

I hold Lydia's hand as we travel the few doors that stand between our house and Dolly's together. Knocking on Dolly's back door I wait, looking down at Lydia with the calendar stretched out in her hands.

"Who is it?" she shouts.

I tell her, realising then it's quite late for Dolly to be having unexpected visitors.

She opens the door, her eyes dropping to see Lydia, gift in hand. She's wearing a cream jumper I haven't seen before with quite a flattering fit. Fur-lined slippers peep out from her dark green trousers so the top half of her looks younger than the bottom half.

"What have you got there then?" she asks, a note of wariness to her tone.

There's only Dolly who would be wary of a small child, bearing gifts.

"We've started Christmas and been to get our tree and my advent calendar with Mr Ralph. I wanted to get him a calendar of his own and I wanted to get one for you too."

She pushes the calendar towards Dolly, and I'm startled when she steps back ever so slightly. I can't understand what could provoke such a reaction. For the third time today I'm struggling to know what to do.

Lydia pushes the calendar nearer, oblivious, and she finally takes it from her.

"A calendar? For me?" she asks.

"Yes, and you can open a door every morning and have a bite of chocolate," Lydia tells her.

Dolly's peering at the calendar in her hand with an odd expression I can't place.

"That's very kind of you both," she tells us without looking up.

Her voice is flat, seeming less than impressed. I wish we hadn't come now, but I thought it was a harmless enough gesture on our part.

"Well, we'll leave you to get back to your evening and I'll go tidy up at home," I say breezily though I feel far from it. I guide Lydia towards the gate.

Dolly nods without smiling, thanking us once more.

"You're welcome," Lydia says and I'm thankful she's blissfully unaware of the frost Dolly has managed to sprinkle on the snow since we arrived. That kind of snow is the most treacherous, and you must tread gingerly. I'm not sure how much more gingerly I can tread though without being unable to move at all.

My mind goes to Ralph; it's obvious he knows more than he's letting on. He almost scurried away up the path like a terrified mouse earlier.

When we get back home, I put Lydia to bed then sit nursing a mug of hot chocolate by the fire. My plan is going awry, I think. Something you can never predict is human reaction, human emotion. I'm not sure now if I gave this enough thought.

The only option open to me now though is to just keep going forward. It's far too late to turn back even if I wanted to because there are so many other people involved. The end is in sight and I'm finally on the cusp of victory.

If not with Dolly, for Wakeley at least.

Chapter 16
Harriet Then

"What time is he coming again?" grandpa asks as I glance at my watch and then the door of *The Crown* for the umpteenth time. The top half of the door has intricately etched glass which states the name of the local brewery, *Tetley's*. The brewery just so happens to be situated less than a hundred yards away.

It enables me to see the outline of anyone entering the pub. I'm poised, ready to spring up from my seat any moment.

"Seven," I tell him, distracted by another customer coming in.

"Well, it's only quarter to by my watch. Settle down," he says, laughing at me, "have a sup of wine to calm your nerves."

I thought it best for them to meet on neutral territory. I'm not sure why that was important, but their meeting must go well. I want them to like each other; in fact, I need them to like each other.

I had a couple of boyfriends at university, but I wouldn't have introduced them to grandpa which eventually made me wonder why. He became a gauge for any future boyfriend's credibility. My flatmates began to couple up, some even seemed lovestruck, so I got carried along on their wave. I wasn't much of a girlfriend if I think back. I was focused and preoccupied with studying, which was unusual, but I was determined not to fritter the opportunity. Not for me and certainly not for gran and grandpa.

I found a weekend call-centre job in Leeds, which gave me an excuse to come home. Looking back, I think this may well have been more for my benefit. I rang grandpa every day, but my homesickness was like a physical pain from Sunday night to Thursday morning when I could see the light at the end of the tunnel for going home. It lessened over the three years admittedly, but it never left.

No, I wasn't much of a catch for anyone back then really.

It was different when I met Daniel, or perhaps first noticed him might be a better description of our first encounter.

That morning as I battled the ever-present wind over Leeds Bridge, my mind was elsewhere as usual, a mental list of tasks loitering permanently in my head. The priority of the tasks switched places like the workings of a complex puzzle I could never quite complete.

I was lucky enough to secure a place at the law firm of Hathersage & Brown. They made me work for it but then I wouldn't expect anything less as they were sponsoring me for my Legal Practice Course. I'd applied after completing my law degree and completed two interviews before the final four-day assessment. Jobs like that were rare as hen's teeth and I was told they'd had around five hundred applications.

When they finally rang to tell me the job was mine, it was a moment to remember. I ended the call, and grandpa and I stood looking at each other a long few seconds before locking arms and jumping up and down with joy in the kitchen.

"I didn't doubt it for a minute," he told me putting the kettle on for tea, which is always the first thing we do after any news, good, bad or indifferent.

I realised eventually he really didn't doubt it. I'd like to bottle his faith in me so I could take a dose of it as required.

I started the job in September, and it was getting towards the end of October by then, but I still felt a fraudster. When I pushed the brass handles on the double oak doors to go inside each morning, I always expected someone to apprehend me. The prestigious old building near the town hall is imposing, a landmark I now call my place of work.

As I rushed along the bridge, I was double-checking I had my entry card and lanyard in the front of my briefcase. I grabbed my usual paper to read at lunchtime. Lunchtimes had to be adhered to no matter how busy we were. It was hard to drag ourselves away from our desk mid-task, but we came back refreshed and that was precisely the reason.

I searched my briefcase to find my purse, jostling with the wind and the newspaper in hand.

"One day you'll get up five minutes earlier, so you have time for a chat," a voice said.

Startled, I looked over my shoulder to see who was being addressed. I saw no-one, so I glanced over the counter to find myself looking into a pair of green eyes. They were twinkling with wry humour.

Those eyes. They were distinctive enough to know I hadn't noticed them before; I would have remembered.

Why hadn't I noticed them, I wondered when I'd grabbed my paper from the same kiosk every workday for the last six weeks? I knew why, I'd been too busy shifting the cogs of my mental puzzle, living in my own head. I'd been striving to make my mark with my new employers.

I couldn't help a smile. I took his bait, his look of delight warming me to the bone.

"Oh, a smile too, it really is my lucky day," he said.

He held out his hand across the stack of newspapers, introducing himself as Daniel.

"Harriet," I said still smiling and shaking his hand with my newly perfected solicitor's handshake, "I'm sorry, I didn't deliberately ignore you. I've started a new job and I'm trying to make myself indispensable."

"Ah, a career-lady," he said, "no time for all that love and stuff I imagine."

I dropped my eyes discovering I was already looking forward to our next encounter the following morning. Our eyes found each other as I dared to look up. His dark hair was curling over the collar of his navy-blue coat that looked expensive, not quite what you might imagine the owner of a small kiosk could afford.

"I'll make sure I set off earlier tomorrow, I promise," I told him, cramming my newspaper into my briefcase.

I offered the money, but he shook his head.

"My treat," he said, "for making my day on this cold autumn morning."

His charming smile immediately set alarm bells ringing in my ears.

"What a schmoozer you are. I bet you say that to all the girls buying a newspaper," I told him, my face on fire.

This is what they call banter, I thought, I need to get better at it. Or perhaps I should just see it as one of the many interludes he has at his kiosk each day.

His smile disappeared as he shook his head.

"Only the one I've been thinking about for weeks, since the first moment I set eyes on her dashing across the bridge towards me. The lady with the auburn hair flying in the wind who seemed to be on some sort of mission. It's taken me all this time to talk to her. I should have done it that first morning and saved myself some sleepless nights.

It wasn't just the wind which took my breath away that October morning.

Funnily enough, I haven't paid for a newspaper since.

*

Here he is, finally, his eyes scouring the room for us.

His broad smile calms me, and I stay seated, the need to jump up like a coiled spring disappearing now he's arrived.

"Grandpa, this is Daniel," I say, "Daniel, Grandpa."

Grandpa makes to stand up, but Daniel gently touches his shoulder and puts his hand out to shake.

"A pleasure, Mr Hargreaves," he says.

"Likewise, lad. What're you having?"

Always the first order of business for grandpa.

"No please, let me, it's my round. Same again?"

We both nod then Daniel weaves his way to the bar. He knows the wine I prefer, and he knows the beer grandpa drinks. He knows plenty about my grandpa.

He's had a haircut for the occasion, but his curls are still intact which I'm glad about.

"You can tell a lot about a fella who stands his round in a pub," grandpa whispers.

"I know, you've told me before. It's one of my strict criteria to be met. You don't think I'd introduce you to any old Tom, Dick or Harry do you, grandpa?"

He chuckles and I realise it must be awkward and strange for him too. I've kept my feelings about Daniel under wraps until recently when I slipped the possibility of meeting up clumsily into the conversation.

Daniel returns with our drinks then takes off his coat and untwirls his scarf. He sits on the stool waiting next to grandpa and I have the seat with the backrest as ladies always have the backrest in grandpa's world. We've managed to get the spot by the fire for once, the coveted spot.

"This is our Harriet's lad," grandpa says to his cronies at the next table. They all smile and nod a greeting as Daniel returns one.

Such a nice introduction. 'Our Harriet's lad' is a pleasant description if a little underdone. Daniel has become far more to me than that, yet it's still taken me over a year to gather us around this table. I wasn't going to play fast and loose with any of our affections.

"So, you've got the kiosk on Leeds bridge, I hear," grandpa says now, "how long have you had it?"

Daniel shoots a quick glance in my direction, clearly thrown by grandpa cutting straight to the chase before he's had chance to take his first sip of beer. He might just as well have asked him about his prospects.

"Only a couple of years. I worked in finance in Manchester before that, but I decided on a change of pace. I live with my brother in Leeds now."

"Why's that then?"

Oh grandpa, I think as Daniel takes a swig of beer, his face unreadable. The inquisition is making me cringe, but I should have realised there would be plenty of questions. Grandpa's approach to life is direct, no-nonsense and straight to the point. It may be quite unnerving to begin with, but then it's like a breath of fresh air. I particularly value it now that I work in an environment where people play games all the time for their own ends … and not only the clients.

"Well, my career got in the way of my relationship, so I made a decision about my priorities."

He pauses, pulling his bottom lip between his thumb and forefinger. It's his tell, a habit he has when he's uncomfortable.

"Sadly, it turned out I was too late in the end."

He's omitting some important facts. Like the fact he was married for five years but his wife was having an affair with an ex for over four of them. That he'd quit his job before he found out to try and get them back on track, so he was then left with nothing in every sense. This would be far too much information for grandpa, for anyone to process at a first meeting.

"So, you learnt the hard way then that there's nothing more important than family," grandpa says, staring into his glass.

His tone holds no judgement only a note of sorrow.

"I did, but I'll not make the same mistake again, Mr Hargreaves, not with Harriet. She might have to be the one to make time for me as it happens."

We laugh together at the irony of his words. I'm learning how to balance my life more. I found it was only a matter of *wanting* to find the balance.

"Call me Robert."

They smile at each other. I know them both well enough to recognise their smiles are genuine and the build-up of tension about the meeting lessens. I silently blow out some air and relax a little.

"I think Daniel can jump off the hot seat grandpa don't you, now you know his intentions are honourable."

He looks non-plussed because he's doing nothing out of the ordinary.

"I understand," Daniel says, lifting his beer, "I know how important you are to each other, and I know why. I wouldn't want to be the one to get in the way of that, even if I could. Cheers to you both."

Clinking glasses, I smile at grandpa, his face ruddy from the beer and the warm fire.

At closing time Daniel gets up to help me with my coat. Grandpa was just about to do it, so he hangs back. I suddenly feel very lucky.

We say our farewells to the regulars and Stan behind the bar then head out into the cold night air. I hug my coat around me, glad we've only a few steps to travel to get home.

"Well, I'm sure I'll be seeing plenty of you so it's a relief our Harriet's been a bit picky," grandpa says shaking his hand.

He bids Daniel a goodnight on his way through the back gate.

"Well, I must say, I'm relieved I passed muster," Daniel says, when he's out of earshot.

"I'll be honest, so am I. I've never introduced him to anyone before because there's no getting away from the fact that he's a hard act to follow."

"I'm glad you don't feel like your compromising," he says now almost shyly.

He glances over the top of the high gate.

"Your house is beautiful, much bigger than I expected," he says.

"I hope you're not after my money, Daniel Scott," I say playfully.

He laughs because he knows I'm joking. He's made plenty of his own again in recent years, especially as he's now content with the simple life. I've always found contentment in it, so this suits me perfectly. He suits me perfectly.

He draws me to him gently with the collar of my coat and we delve into the depths of each other's eyes for a moment. I feel raw, exposed as I kiss him under the streetlight, allowing myself to sink into the pleasure of him for a little while. I'd never known a real kiss until I met Daniel.

We don't wear rose-tinted glasses around one another. There's been the odd bickering session over the last year about silly things. He thinks I don't know how to relax, and he's retrained himself to be good at it. I like that we're not too perfect, it makes me less wary of failure. Lying awake one night I summed up my love for him as one of purity, of clarity. I'm safe being vulnerable with Daniel.

He waves to me from the bridge as he makes his way home. One bridge stood between us for years, just one little bridge.

When I go inside grandpa is sitting in the kitchen, the teapot steaming in the middle of the table. I slide my feet into my slippers waiting on the hearth.

As I sit in my chair on the opposite side of the table, I'm full of anticipation. We've kept the same places from me being a little girl, living our ups and downs of life together around a square of polished oak with four legs.

He knows what I'm thinking, but his face remains solemn. Finally, it breaks into a mischievous grin.

"He'll do," he says.

High praise indeed, never being one to over-egg the pudding when it comes to sentimentality.

"You can set a place for him at Christmas if you like."

My jaw hangs at such a gesture. This is the royal seal of approval from my grandfather.

"So, you clearly like the cut of his gib then?" I ask, pouring the tea.

As it happens, grandpa did like it. He liked it enough to give consent to Daniel marrying me six months later, to have him move in with us and share our life, to share the affections of his adored granddaughter and eventually great granddaughter. Enough to bring him on board with *Operation Dolly* as we affectionately termed it.

He was instrumental in making it real, making it work for all of us with his old contacts, but more importantly in practical terms.

And on more than a few occasions, he was even prepared to play second fiddle to a woman he'd never even set eyes on.

It's fair to say I like the cut of his gib too.

Chapter 17
Harriet Now

People must put their trees up late here. Ours is still the only one on display. Every window is treeless not just on our row but in the whole town.

It's dark by the time I leave the town hall to go home and there's no indication yet that the festivities will be arriving in two weeks-time. They start late in Wakeley by the look of it. Ralph hasn't put his tree up yet either and I know Lydia will have been badgering the life out of him. It's all giving me a terrible sense of unease.

I admit I've been preoccupied. My mind hasn't been entirely on Christmas for once because I have important matters on the horizon, ones I've worked long and hard to achieve. I think I've managed to hide my growing agitation quite well considering. I never know if I'm able to do this by nature or nurture, but I've never been more thankful for it.

So, today's the day. Today is the day all the strands of my plan come together to hopefully weave one strong, invincible weft. Now, I just need a little pinch of luck, although nothing has been left to chance; everything is ready and waiting for me to finally do what I must do.

I'm well acquainted with public speaking; it goes with the job and my powers of persuasion are honed. My quiet nature often means this skill can come as something of a surprise.

But I'm not speaking on behalf of a client today, I'm speaking on behalf of my grandfather's hometown and more to the point, the town's most beloved lifelong resident.

I hang up my coat and head to the council chamber of the town hall to check again I haven't forgotten anything. The building has that slightly foisty smell old buildings exude, a layering of stagnant drains, imbedded dirt, human life, and the usual ravages of time. It's not unpleasant and I've grown used to it, so it's become barely noticeable over the last few months. Today however my senses are heightened.

I left work late last night and I've arrived early today. Ralph said he'd have breakfast with us so I could get a head start. I know I'm over-preparing but I'm not spoiling the ship for an ha'porth of tar, as grandpa would say. I fill the water jugs in the kitchen then position them both ends of the long table.

I thought about doing an electronic presentation, but everyone knows individually what it is I have in mind. There's been enough meetings over the last few years to stake my claims.

So, after much deliberation, I've decided to speak to the gathering without notes. I decided the best option, now I've given them all the cold hard facts, is to just simply speak from the heart.

I've known Bernie the longest as he was the first person I contacted in Wakeley around two years ago now. We must start somewhere, and I thought the first party I needed on my side was the council. Bernie was an old-time councillor, punch drunk from endless setbacks and false promises. Tired and disengaged, he was symbolic of the whole ethos of the town. It was then I realised the magnitude of the task ahead of me.

Daniel asked me once if I'd ever thought about throwing in the towel. I hadn't, but once he'd brought it to my attention I wondered why.

Now I know it's because I've been propelled by the people in my mother and grandparent's story, people who became my story. I've been blessed with grandpa's dogged determination and knowing I had the tools to help them … and I want to, for them but also for me. I hear talk of there being no such thing as an unselfish act as you also benefit from the satisfaction. There's no arguing that point, but surely two positives can never make a negative whichever way you look at it.

That first day with Bernie I sat with him for three hours or more drinking tea in his office while I explained my convoluted plan. The whole time I was there I knew what he was thinking: what does this young lass have to offer us? Ralph had put a good word in for me, but I could tell he thought I was well-meaning but deluded. I expected it. I would have been surprised if he hadn't been sceptical. You can only get to know someone steadily over time to be sure about their character. I was in no rush.

Admittedly he was impressed at the legwork I'd already done. So, by the end of the meeting he was little more convinced and prepared to humour me at least, and he knew I had contacts. He told me to come back when I'd got all the strands of the project pulled together and we would talk again. The next meeting took place over a year ago and we've come a long way since then.

Up hill and down dale.

In between the meetings I was busy, spurred on more by Bernie's scepticism perhaps. I contacted the owner of *Lumley's* dairy, Graham Lumley, then potential investors and town landlords including Jonny Pritchard. I researched every possible source of funding from local and national government to the lottery and venture capitalists, filling in countless applications, one after another. Rejections came in steadily, but some were prepared to give support in principle. My theory was the more applications I submitted, the better chance I had of achieving the estimated fund total.

However, the response from each party after months of correspondence, meetings and discussion was always the same. They would be on board they said, if I could get the other parties to agree. I was caught in a loop, going round in circles.

So now, in thirty minutes, I'll have all the people who I've tried to convince individually gathered under one roof. This is it, it's now or never … crunch time.

If I can't seal the deal, I'll have to take the long walk to Dolly's house with my tail between my legs. I'll have to tell her who I am. I'll have to sit through the galling conversation about why I came here and what Ive been doing all this time, but with nothing to show for it.

Bernie knows how much is depending on today and not just for me but for him personally and for Wakeley. He knows my success will be the town's success. The options have been growing fewer and fewer, even in the time since we first met and Wakeley is dropping further and further down everyone's list of priorities. It's like they've given up on it.

"Sometimes we see the light for ourselves, sometimes we need someone to shove us outside to have a look," he told me recently. He was clearly annoyed with himself and his lack of vision.

Though he and his wife are still living here, his three children and seven grandchildren are scattered across the country as his town has nothing to offer other than the limited opportunities of *Lumley's*. He's not as lazy as people think, and I couldn't blame him for being demotivated after so many disappointments. In the end though I'm glad I was able to lead him to the water and now he's prepared to drink it. Credit where its due.

I couldn't see the point in not disclosing who I was to Bernie. It made sense so he knew why Wakeley was and is so important to me when there are other towns in a similar position. I just asked if we could keep it under wraps until we had everything finalised. He readily agreed because he didn't want to raise peoples' hopes for nothing.

A sharp knock on the door startles me. I check my watch; half past nine. Carol, Bernie's part-time secretary come finance administrator, pops her head around the door to inform us Reverend Burton has arrived.

I scan the room one final time. The hot refreshments are waiting, and I've organised a small buffet at lunchtime. The room is tired but clean and functional, much like Wakeley.

I heave a breath and glance at Bernie who has already jumped up from his seat to put on his suit jacket. His salt and pepper beard has been given a fresh trim for the occasion and he looks groomed and ready; all set for one final fight for his hometown.

Oh, how my heart swells.

"Right, let's do this," Bernie says, pushing up his tie, "show him in Carol, will you please?"

I feel dizzy and more than a little sick but that's just too bad. I push my shoulders back and smooth my hair, performing the rituals I go through when preparing for my closing speeches in court.

"You've got this, Harriet Ann Scott, you've got this," I murmur to myself.

"I've been thinking, it's a nice touch Harriet, for you to pick today of all days to hold the meeting," he says.

I shake my head, bemused but there's no time to ask what he's referring to as the door reopens and the vicar appears, smiling as he bounds towards us. He's full of vigour and excitement and my confidence brims at the sight of him.

One after another they drift in. One after another, the people who will determine our destiny arrive to listen to what I have to say. It must be good.

The meeting starts at ten, so I've time to talk to each of them over tea and coffee about their partners, their children, their dogs, their lives. I know some of them very well, some less so, but enough for them to be invested in my vision at least.

The town hall clock strikes at precisely ten o'clock as it should, and Bernie asks everyone to join us around the long table. The small groups disband, and our guests sit down still talking quietly amongst themselves.

A hush steadily descends on the room, changing the atmosphere; business is afoot. Closing my eyes briefly I take a sip of water as Bernie officially opens the meeting and goes through the housekeeping details.

I'm tuned out, mentally preparing for my presentation with key words lining up in my head like soldiers.

I hear him say, "But it's not all about me for once," there's a small ripple of laughter, "so I'll hand you over to Harriet Scott who I know needs no further introduction."

A stark silence descends to terrify me. I take a final deep breath and Bernie pats my hand under the table. I glance up at him and then at the other men and women gathered at my request. Everyone's smiling at me, waiting to see what I have to say. I smile tentatively back at them, it's enough to settle my nerves so I can go on.

Shoulders back, I walk to the front of the room. It's just me as planned, no laptop, no notes to hide behind. In the hush of the room, I search and find my first words.

I am now as ready as I will ever be.

"If you'll indulge me a moment, I'd like to explain why today is such a momentous day for me."

I scan the faces turned my way, listening intently.

"I never knew my mother. Her life ended as mine began, but I came to know her so well through the charming letters of a certain lady named Dolly Hunter whom some of you know. For those of you who don't, Dolly has lived in Wakeley all her life and was my mother's best friend, even after she had to move away to be closer to the hospital. My mother was bedridden for some time in her teenage years due to a heart problem. She went on to have an operation and fall in love with my father but during that lonely, worrisome time, Dolly visited my mother every single day. This thought always brings me comfort.

When I was seventeen and my grandmother had just died, my grandfather told me a story. My grandmother didn't celebrate Christmas so, what others take for granted I never knew. My grandfather, Robert Hargreaves had always wanted me to have a Christmas to remember and he made sure I had one. I've had one every year since."

I witness the penny dropping on some of the faces at the mention of grandpa's name. He's a local legend, much like Eric Hunter.

"One Christmas Eve by the fireside, he told me the story of Dolly's father, his best friend Eric, and the terrible day of the *Worthington's* fire. How Eric's heroism was hidden and unrecognised thanks to the betrayal of a so-called friend; and how, during that time, Dolly and her mother had to live with the shame of thinking he had caused the fire and risked the lives of hundreds of colleagues and friends.

This story completed the mental jigsaw I'd created and brought to life the stories and the people so vividly described in Dolly's letters to my mother. Though I'd never met her, Dolly became a role model in my life.

I'm hoping now perhaps you'll understand how significant Dolly is to me. I cared deeply about her well-being before I even knew her. Still a teenager myself, albeit one who had been forced to grow up quicker than most through circumstance, that Christmas I made a decision: I was going to find some way to repay Dolly for all her kindness to my family and for all the hardship she had endured. It has become my mission in life, almost to the point of obsession.

I'm now thirty-four years old and I've been working slowly but surely towards my goal ever since that night.

As some of you know, the fire wasn't the end of *Worthington's* by any means. The building was repaired, and the business recovered. In fact, it went from strength to strength, and it was ironically this success which brought Wakeley to its knees."

Everyone appears to be still engaged, however ,I know from experience I must end my trip down memory lane and come to the point soon before I lose my audience.

"But we're not here today for sentimentality, we're here today for business."

There's a silent acknowledgement of the change in tone as backs straighten ready for full steam ahead.

"You have in front of you the proposal I've put together. I've spoken to you individually about this and I know some of you have your doubts, which is entirely understandable. One thing I know for certain: there isn't anyone in this room who doesn't want to get Wakeley back on its feet and to see it thriving again. Thriving so its young people don't have to go off to Leeds for work and decent housing. Wakeley deserves better and its people deserve better. Now is the time to start making it happen."

I pause and you could cut the silence with a knife. Everyone is looking at me intently, and Bernie and the vicar have the same expression grandpa used to have on his face when he watched me sing in a choir.

"Fine words and sentiments won't better any parsnips as my Grandpa always said. So, let's get down to business and go over this proposal in detail."

All hands reach for their copy of the document and turn the cover page together as though we're running through a script at first rehearsal.

"We start with *Lumley's*," I say, smiling at Graham, who returns a warm smile.

"*Lumley's* is expanding," I announce and let the statement hang in the air, floating around us to finally settle. This fact I know needs maximum impact.

There are some audible gasps and people turn to their neighbour with a quizzical expression. I plough on, seizing the moment.

"They have secured investment backing to expand their production capacity. This would be no small expansion; it would be to supply the whole of the north of England and potentially beyond in the future.

People around here already know the exceptional quality of their dairy products and with the right branding—built around the family run business—and the new investment in their Wakeley site, they can become a major player in the UK and international markets. They have already secured a new contract with a national supermarket chain, and meetings with others are in the pipeline.

Lumley's are the lynchpin of the plan and Graham ad his team are fully on board with the opportunity."

The change in atmosphere is palpable. Where once was just a dream, an idea, now there is substance, a plan, a solid, real foundation to build on. Graham raises his eyebrows, telling me he feels it too. He's almost glowing with pride at my announcement.

Alongside Bernie, I know Graham best. After our first formal meeting in his office, we've since met many times in his cosy farmhouse kitchen, his wife and teenage children busying themselves around us. He knows he's at the centre of the whole deal and after a little persuasion, he's excited about how Lumley's growth and Wakeley's rebirth are mutually beneficial and go hand in hand. He confessed he'd been concerned about what would become of *Lumley's* after he retired when he'd been throwing good money after bad for many a year.

I'd had years of managing the family groceries with grandpa, and I know people want the best quality at an affordable price and drew confidence from the idea of a traditional, family run brand. I introduced Graham to some clients who were business backers. They were looking for a strong growth opportunity in the food retail sector; a respected brand with opportunities to grow with the right backing. It was a perfect fit.

"The expansion of *Lumley's* would of course provide significant employment opportunities; and this in turn will act as the catalyst and cornerstone of further investment in the town. Graham has been incredibly generous and is prepared to release the land to the east of the current site on Thorndale Road, which was the site of the first *Lumley's* dairy, for new housing.

Thorndale Council has indicated it will look favourably on the re-designation of the land for housing when a planning application is submitted, as this supports their plans for economic regeneration…but there is a condition…"

Shoulders which have been pressed further and further back as I speak sag momentarily.

"…that permission will be conditional on the renovation of Wakeley's older housing stock. The landlords I've spoken to now see this as an opportunity not to be missed and are open to the possibility of houses being sold.

New people will help to revive the town's economy allowing retail, the church, and the environment to thrive. Eventually the school could be reopened, even the pub and the library.

Derek Ibbotson from the Government's *Regional Growth Fund* who has given approval in principle to an application for grants is here to talk to you today."

Derek nods to the people around the table.

"But before I hand over to Derek, there is one more vital piece of the jigsaw we haven't spoken of, " I declare, pausing for attention and emphasis.

"I'd like to paint a picture of how wonderful it would be to see *Worthies*, the heart and soul of this town restored to its rightful place.

It's days as a working copper mill are part of Wakeley's past now, but some of us believe there is an opportunity to re-launch the impressive *Worthington's* site as a museum with funding from the Lottery and *Thorndale Industrial Heritage Society*. The building and machinery have been maintained by the council so renovation would be minimal."

I pause to take a sip of water and give myself enough time to catch my breath before I go on.

"I know this isn't going to happen overnight and there is a mountain of work still to do, but this is a long-term plan. Wakeley needs to learn how to walk again first.

I hope you will see that this isn't some half-baked, hare-brained scheme as my grandpa would say. I've been working steadfastly towards this goal for almost seventeen years. This is a solid business proposition and the support I've already secured is real, very real. Where once I used to think it could happen for the town, the very fact you are all here today makes me certain it *can* happen.

My dream could be our reality.

Now I'm sure many of you will be thinking: what's in this for me; why have I been so dedicated to the cause?

Well, I certainly won't be receiving any monetary reward. But now you know the backstory I hope you understand that although I'm not from Wakeley, it has become my home from home. I've grown to care about the people here, some have become like family but it's so much more than that. These people deserve it. They deserve to have the legacy of their town live on because there aren't many left like them if we're all honest with ourselves. People who have suffered not just for a while but for years but would still give you their last penny. People who are weary but good and kind-hearted. True gentlefolk."

My voice which sounded so clear and composed, breaks on the very last word. I'm thinking of Ralph, Bernie, Graham, Sally, Mrs Turrell and of course Dolly. I'm thinking of the ones who were such a huge part of the town who moved away through no choice of their own like grandpa; as well as the ones who are no longer with us; my gran, Dolly's mother and father and my own extraordinary mother.

I'm disappointed in myself for wavering and appearing sentimental in front of such influential business investors. These are my own private thoughts and my own reason to succeed, not to be shared in this environment.

I keep my eyes lowered, trying to pull myself together. As I head back to my seat, I'm admonishing myself because it was all going so well, I could sense it. Now I've disclosed too much, just when the finishing line was in sight. It was right there within my grasp.

The silence is gripping me too tightly. I'd like to gather my things and leave now I've said what I came to say, but that's impossible.

A chair scrapes across the wooden floorboards. It echoes around the room and then it's joined by the sound of more chairs. I look up to see Graham scrabbling to his feet. Bernie joins him, then the vicar, and eventually everyone else.

Graham looks me straight in the eyes and I'm suddenly exposed and hanging out to dry.

Then he begins to clap, loudly and steadily. I'm not sure what's happening but then others join him so my eyes whip around the table watching all the people I've grown to care about and admire on their feet clapping and beaming their smiles in my direction. The cacophony in the high-ceilinged boardroom is deafening.

Tears blur my eyes, and I blink and swallow hard to control the flow. I'm overcome with pride but most of all with relief.

As long as I live, I shall never forget this feeling, I think.

It appears after years of waiting and wondering, *Operation Dolly* has just this very minute been stamped with one almighty seal of approval.

Chapter 18

The icy air stings my throat as I make my way down the steps of the town hall. I scrabble for my gloves in my bag then tighten my scarf to curb the coldness.

"We've got this you know, Harriet," Bernie tells me, and I smile at him thinking about the mantra I was repeating to myself only hours ago.

"I know it will seem like an age until we get everything signed off on the legal front, but you did it. I hope you're proud of yourself, Mrs Scott."

"We did it," I say, "but perhaps it's a little premature for celebrations, Bernie."

It's the truth and not false modesty; I really couldn't have done it without him. He arranged for me to rent the house and paved the way with Graham and the vicar, so I wasn't a cold caller.

"There's still the planning meeting with the council. I've put the notices in your bottom tray for tomorrow. Thank you for speaking on my behalf at the next meeting, I don't think I could go through all that again."

I know I couldn't.

"As agreed, I'm still telling them who you are though and why you're doing all this?" he asks.

I nod saying, "There's no context otherwise, Bernie and word will soon get around. It's better coming from you and Graham because they know and trust you. I'm just a random stranger who appeared from nowhere one day."

He lets out a low laugh, shaking his head.

"You're hardly a stranger any more from what I hear."

Coming to a standstill at his car he turns to face me.

"You know, your oratory skills are second to none Harriet, but there's one person I wouldn't like to have to test them on."

He's obviously referring to Dolly. My stomach drops at the thought of our looming encounter, then I remember something he said earlier.

"What did you mean when you mentioned about picking today of all days to hold the meeting?" I ask him.

He unlocks his car and throws his briefcase on the front passenger seat.

"Well, you know, with it being fifty years today since the accident. I thought it was so poignant."

Did I hear correctly I wonder; fifty years ago today, the man said. So, it appears I haven't thought of everything after all. Why hadn't this crucial fact occurred to me when the date of the tragedy is imprinted on my mind?

"Oh, I see what you mean," I say, backing away from Bernie and the conversation, "Well, thanks again for all your support, Bernie, I'll see you later in the week. I must get back and relieve Ralph; Lydia will be chewing his ear off."

I scoot off quickly towards home, waving to Bernie as he leaves the carpark. I'll be glad when I'm in the house now and I can close the door on the world.

What a day I've had to say the least.

As I reach the first row of houses, I stop in my tracks, feeling my lower lip drop.

All down the road and beyond there's a candle burning in every inhabited house. The ghostly sight of them flickering against the darkness takes my breath away.

The significance dawns on me immediately. I take great gulps of frosty air, so it burns all the way down to my chest. I think of our tree blazing merrily away in the window for two weeks. Oh, the shame.

That's why Ralph hasn't put his tree up, why he's been acting out of character, it's all falling into place as I watch the candles mocking me.

I can't go home now. Not yet, but I can't risk Joyce Pinner watching me from her window either. I'm suddenly trapped with nowhere to turn.

So, my only option is to run around the back of the empty town hall. My shoes on the cobbles are the only sound and it's difficult to see as there's one exterior light and it hasn't worked since I've been here. I sit on the second step of the rear entrance and drop my head into my hands.

Then there in the blackness of the carpark I start to cry. I cry like I haven't cried for many years.

Not since the night long ago when my lovely gran finally gave up her brutal slog to stay with us and died in my arms.

*

Ralph's playing table-top football with Lydia when I finally get home.

Walking past the candlelit houses was torturous and the first thing I do when I get in the door is draw the curtains. The tree now seems like a garish insult, a giant two fingers to Dolly and Walkley.

"Hi, mum," Lydia says, her eyes fixed firmly on the game.

"Hi, sunshine, looks like you're having fun. Thanks for today, Ralph," I say, keeping my head down.

He looks up from the game briefly saying, "No problem, hope …" his voice tails off when despite my best efforts to hide it, he spots my tearstained face.

I'm thankful for the distraction of my daughter. Ralph brought the old football game over for them to play with when the weather prevents them playing outside. He's had it since he was a boy and it's been well-used. They're both as obsessed as each other.

I head into the kitchen to start tea. Ralph doesn't need an invitation to stay for tea nowadays.

When I come back downstairs after putting Lydia to bed, he's finishing off the washing up. It looks like he's already stoked the fire because it's roaring up the back. His quiet presence is like a warm blanket at the end of a taxing day.

"Sit down before you fall down, lass," he says, wiping his hands on the tea towel.

I don't need telling twice. I fall onto the sofa and drop my head back onto the cushion with a sigh, suddenly drained of all energy.

"It didn't go well, I take it," he says.

I pull my legs up under me and pull my hair out of its tight bun in the hope it will make me relax a little.

"It couldn't have gone better, Ralph to be honest."

"Well good, I'm glad to hear it, but you need to tell your face."

I look at him standing over me, his face full of concern.

"I don't understand why you didn't tell me," I say my voice quiet and hoarse.

Sighing, he sits down in what I now think of as his chair by the fire.

"Ah, I see now," he says, "you've found out then."

"You should have said, Ralph, I feel a complete and utter fool."

He sits back in his seat and stares at me so long I start to feel uncomfortable for once.

"It was quite simple, Hattie," he says finally, "I wanted you to do what you needed to, without the chains of our long sadness holding you back. I wanted you to come with a clean slate to show us all what we've been missing."

So, that's why. It's understandable, but it means I've been stomping over peoples' feelings like a bull in a china shop when all I wanted was to help them get back on their feet.

"I would have picked a different day," I tell him.

His brow creases and he shakes his head at me.

"A different day? I thought you were talking about the candles. I had it in my head that you'd picked today deliberately for the significance of it. I didn't realise."

So, Ralph thought the same as Bernie it seems. But that's not my only concern.

"What about the tree, Ralph? You bought one too, you went along with it when you clearly didn't want to."

"No, I didn't want to at first, you're right, but I did it for you and for the little lass. I'm glad I bought it, but I can't put it up until I've spoken to Dolly. Truth is nobody has had a tree in their window since 1973."

I sit bolt upright panic-stricken as I realise the implication of what I've done.

"Nobody has lit a tree for fifty years. Fifty years! I can't believe it, Ralph. Why did you let me disrespect Dolly like that, disrespect the whole town even? I've swept in and put up a huge tree for all to see in my window from the beginning of December. Everyone has walked past it every day, including Dolly, and thought who knows what about me. Dolly must be mortified."

Ralph holds his hand up to stem my babbling; I'm getting on the wrong side of hysteria. It's too late in the day for this conversation in every respect.

"Calm down, lass. Dolly will have thought plenty, I'm sure, but she hasn't said anything. She will know you didn't do it to spite her. The same goes for the advent calendar. How were you to know? It's none of mine, Dolly's or anybody else's business how you and your family keep Christmas and you meant no harm by it. It's long overdue anyway if you ask me. When I've spoken to Dolly tomorrow, I'm going to put my tree in the window. As Lydia said, my house has looked sad for too many years and so has the whole town. I know most people put a tree up, they just don't put it in the window. They enjoy it when the curtains are drawn, and the candles are lit. It's ridiculous after all these years, but to be fair to her, Dolly didn't ask them to do it."

His face is red from making his point so earnestly.

No, Dolly didn't ask them to do it, I think but they wanted to do it. They did it out of love and respect.

I glance at our unlit tree thinking I shall never feel the same way about it now.

"Now listen to me, Harriet Ann Scott and listen well. You came here of your own accord to save a lady who you'd never met, and in turn save a town on its last legs. How many people in the world would even think to do that, never mind put the wheels in motion? How many people in the world would spend year after year planning to drag a town kicking and screaming into the twenty first century? Dolly's not daft, she knows her life can't stay the same forever, that the future's looking bleaker every day. There's plenty of people left who we care about, and it's been hard watching the steady decline of something you love, watching people move away because they've no option. We've become used to it, but that's not right. You've shown me that's not right. So, you think you picked the wrong day to do it. Did you ever stop to think it might be the perfect day? That fate had stepped in to say, after fifty years, enough is enough?"

Oh, Ralph, I think, you've been on my side since the first telephone conversation five years or more ago. I knew I could trust you before I'd even spoken to you, which says so much.

"I've pushed too hard, Ralph. I feel like telling Bernie to cancel the planning meeting."

"Hattie, you haven't pushed too hard, love, I've never heard a wrong word said about you both. You're a breath of much needed fresh air around here and they'll be as excited for a new start as I am when they find out. I know it; I can already sense the change in people I've known my whole life."

"Perhaps I should have spoken to Dolly first."

Ralph splutters and moves to the edge of his seat.

"Have you lost your marbles? If I thought for one minute that was the right way around, I would have said. She'd have sent you off with a flea in your ear for having such highfalutin ideas, Margaret's lass or not."

I laugh out loud, and he joins in. A valve is released as my laughing grows louder until I think I won't stop, and I sound like I'm losing my mind.

"Whoa," Ralph says, "steady now, it wasn't that funny."

I close my eyes and breath heavily until I get myself under control.

"Well, Mr Ralph, we'll just have to put our head down and keep going then. I suppose we've come too far to turn back and there's not just us to think about any longer. I need to speak to Dolly tomorrow. The planning meeting notices are going up the day after and I have my own deadline to meet as I must get back to work. I was lucky they let me take a sabbatical for a year."

"Lucky be beggared. They wanted you to come back to them not some other firm who would reap the benefits. They know a good thing when they see it."

I manage to raise a smile for him.

"And I'll tell you another thing for nothing; Dolly Hunter loves that little lass as much as I do. We had a trump card there. If you weren't such a bag of nerves around her, she'd feel the same about you too. I've never met anyone like you and that's the plain, honest truth."

I look down at the rug, the heat rising up my neck. I can't help glowing with pride because this man has become so much more than a friend.

Ralph gets up and takes his coat from the rack at the bottom of the stairs as I join him to say goodnight.

"The next step is going to be the hardest, harder than today in another way, I know I don't have to tell you as much. This is Dolly we're talking about; she doesn't drop her defences easily, not anymore."

He gazes over my shoulder into the fire.

"And I wish you'd tell her how you feel," I say, holding his forearm, "one thing I do know is Dolly's tough, not hard and there's a big difference. I have a vibe you might not get short shrift if you opened your heart, especially if she discovered she was the reason you returned to Wakeley. I can't believe you've managed to keep that little bombshell under wraps. Now I ask you, is this remarkable discretion, or a waste of two lives? Only you have the answer to that one."

He snorts and heads into the kitchen, turning to face me when he reaches the door with his hand resting on the handle.

"Tough, hard, whatever, there's too much water gone under the bridge for all that. I don't know, Hattie, we haven't done this the easy way, have we?" he says, looking down at me.

I reach up and drop a light kiss on his cheek. The smell of his soap grounds me and makes me think of grandpa. Ralph's coy smile melts my heart, and my throat tightens at the thought of the two men who have given me so much.

"Remember, we've always had the best of intentions," he says over his shoulder as he heads down the back yard.

I close the door and sigh as I look around our cosy little kitchen. It really has become a home from home, it wasn't just words.

Daniel and grandpa will be waiting for my video call. Worn out or not, it will be a long chat tonight.

As I settle down by the fire with my phone, Ralph's final words are bouncing around my head.

I know he meant well, but I can't help but think that the long road to hell is paved with good intentions.

Chapter 19

"Good luck!" I shout to Ralph and Lydia as they head off for the last match before Christmas. Lydia's holding his hand and Ralph's carrying her kit bag over his shoulder.

"Thanks, mum, see you soon," she shouts, waving.

"And you!" Ralph calls, and I know what he's thinking.

I watch them a while as they cross the road and head towards the old school, looking like they've known each other forever. I wish Ralph was coming with me, but his turn to talk to Dolly is later, and I needed a diversion for Lydia. I'll have to get my skates on if I'm going to catch her before she leaves to watch the match. I rush out the back door, weaving my way down my back path, along the ginnel and up Dolly's path.

Twice I raise my hand to knock and then think better of it. I take a deep breath and raise it again, only for it to drop to my side of its own accord once more.

I lean against Dolly's limewashed yard wall and look up at the grey sky. I can't do it, I think. Everything's riding on this conversation and I just can't face the consequences.

I'm startled now by the door suddenly opening. Dolly's mouth drops when she sees me loitering in her back yard and I feel like a child who's been caught doing something they shouldn't. She has that effect on me. She's muffled up in her warmest clothes for the match and I noticed a few weeks ago she's seen sense and progressed to fur-lined wellington boots. I stare at them now as I can't look up.

"What the blazes?" she says, "Is something up with the bairn; Ralph?"

I take a deep gulp of air then blow it out slowly. I look up and meet her eye as she shakes her head with impatience.

"No, Dolly, they're both on their way already. I'm taking the opportunity to come and talk to you."

Her eyes are full of suspicion suddenly and they bore a hole in mine as she stares at me. A shiver runs from the top of my spine to the bottom and not from the cold weather.

"Well, you better come in then," she says, pulling the door open wider to let me pass.

I don't want to keep her waiting any longer, so I step quickly over the threshold. I take off my boots, placing them neatly on the rack in the kitchen and she pulls off her boots to join them.

"Tea?" she asks.

I don't know what the right answer is to the question. I'm not sure if tea will make everything better for once, or if it will prolong my agony while I wait for her to make it. I decide on the latter.

"No, I'm fine, thank you, I've just had one."

"Go through then, the fire will still be high."

I wander into her elegant front room and wait for her to nod at a chair.

"Take your coat off, or you'll not feel the benefit," she says, and I slide my arms out but keep it at the back of me. Dolly hangs her coat on the back of her chair neatly.

She sits back down opposite me but doesn't speak. I'd like to bolt out of the front door, almost itching with the temptation.

She's still holding her nerve waiting for me to start the conversation. Come on, Harriet I think, take the first step before you rattle her any further.

"Dolly, forgive me I'm very nervous so I hope my words come out in the right order," I say with a funny, little laugh.

"Well, this all seems very serious I must say. What have you to be nervous about?" she asks.

Her tone is withering though the words aren't unkind.

"Firstly, I must apologies for putting my Christmas tree up. If I'd known I wouldn't have, believe me."

She shrugs dismissively.

"Why would you know? In any case a person is entitled to put up a Christmas tree if they want to, it's none of my business."

I look down at my hands folded in my lap. I realise I'm sitting in the same way as when I'm in an interview situation.

"Well, I knew some of what happened to your family but I'd no idea it was fifty years ago yesterday. I feel very tactless."

"There's no need for an apology but I accept it regardless," she says, "but you said "firstly," so I'm waiting to find out more about why you're here."

I notice the dancing snowman chocolate advent calendar on the shelf in the alcove. Many doors are open and empty, and I wonder if she had the chocolate or Lydia.

"Right, well, it's like this. You see, I didn't pluck Wakeley out of thin air as I might have led you to believe. I have connections with the town. Strong connections, family ones in fact."

She stares at me, her eyes narrowing slightly.

"There's no easy way to tell you this Dolly, so I'll do us both a favour and just spit it out," I pause but only briefly because I know there's no turning back, "I'm the daughter of Margaret Hargreaves."

She pulls her neck backwards and her mouth opens and closes a few times, lost for words. I decide it might be best to plough on.

"Robert is my grandfather, and he lives with my husband Daniel, Lydia and I in the house I grew up in near Leeds. We converted the attic so he could live with us independently. He's fine and very alert for his age."

I'm talking too quickly now, using silly little details to mask the awkwardness of the situation.

"I see, well I'm very pleased to hear it," she says, more than a hint of frostiness in her voice, "Robert and your mother were a very big part of my life ... but I'm telling you something you already know. You have me at disadvantage."

"I know, and I can only apologise. I felt I knew you and Ralph before I even arrived in Wakeley. The thing is, on my thirteenth birthday my grandpa gave me the letters you wrote to my mum before she died. I treasure them ... particularly as I never had the chance to meet her."

Dolly gets to her feet and walks past me to stand by the window. She has her back to me, staring out of the window onto the street. Now I'm unable to read her expression which no doubt was her intention.

"I don't understand," she says, after a moment, "why all the cloak and dagger, why not just call in for a cup of tea and a natter?"

I heave a deep breath and close my eyes briefly.

"Ralph kept in touch with grandpa, and I knew the town was struggling after the closure of the copperworks."

"Oh, he did, did he?" she says sarcastically, "No doubt Ralph has taken it upon himself to tell you plenty more about me."

I'm calmer now she's not looking at me, and a little stronger in spirit. I've thought of every way this conversation might play out over the years.

"No, Ralph only speaks very highly of you. Perhaps in hindsight I should have just called in for a chat with you, but I've had this big idea brewing for years to thank my grandpa for all he's done for me and to thank you for all you did for mum. I wanted to do it properly on their behalf and make a real difference."

"What do you mean by big idea?" she asks, her shoulders raising slightly. She's ready to draw her sword and do battle, I can tell even without seeing her face.

"I don't want it to sound like I'm full of myself because Ralph will tell you I'm not, but I happen to be a solicitor with good contacts and over the years I've been putting plans in place to help Wakeley get back on track."

She glances over her shoulder at me now, her face set and pale in the light from the window.

"Help Wakeley; in what way can you help us?"

So, I tell her about the years of planning and negotiations which have been held. I tell her about the possibility of the dairy expansion, the housing and regeneration and everything else which is waiting on a plate. All the while she listens without interruption, her gaze steady.

I finish my pitch and she remains silent for too long. She turns to look back out of the window, so I have a stab of rejection.

"I didn't want to just know you, Dolly, I wanted to secure your future if I could. I don't want you to think I had ideas above my station, but I didn't want to get your hopes up if I couldn't make it happen."

Sighing, I make a last-ditch attempt at getting her to at least engage.

"And most of all I just wanted you to like me despite who my mother was. It seems ridiculous now."

Still, she won't face me.

"You say there's a meeting about it at the town hall next week?"

This is it. This is my moment, the opportunity to tell her about the crux of all the planning.

"Yes, but listen to me, you are the one with all the power, Dolly. If you don't want it to happen it won't. That was my thinking the whole time. The town would never do anything you didn't want to do. I know how much they care about you. I understand why they do."

She spins around as though she's about to lunge at me, so I lean back in my chair.

"How can you possibly understand? You haven't been here two minutes. Sixty- four years I've lived in this house. Sixty-four bloody years!" she yells, "What the hell gives you the right to plan my life for me behind my back; to even assume I want it changing in the first place?"

Though I'm shaken by her vitriolic tone I rise and stand firm, strength appearing from somewhere just when I need. I ignore her thunderous expression because this might be my last chance. I must make it count.

"What if something happens to Ralph?" I ask, "What if you become unwell? The town is falling down around you, Dolly, but you could live here forever if we rebuilt it. You deserve it, so do the other residents. So does Ralph."

"Him! He's worse than you are. He's always been swung by a pretty face. Swanning in here and telling me I need to do this for the future of the town, that for the future of the town. It's my town and my life, not yours. You're welcome to each other, I tell you. He's betrayed me even more than you have."

Her eyes are on fire, her face puce with anger as she glowers at me. It's a terrifying sight and this is no overstatement. But I must cling onto my tenacity and persevere. If I'm to lose, I must go down fighting my cause.

"He hasn't betrayed you he's done all this for you, for both of you and your friends here. You go back a long way, and he cares very deeply about you."

I could say more, but that's not my secret to share. I'm not sure now if my vibe was on target after all.

I take one step nearer but then I can't bring myself to go any further.

"Dolly, I've told you my reasons for not telling you and perhaps you will never forgive me but please don't shoot yourself in the foot because of it. The opportunity is there for you to take, for the whole town to take, but only if *you* want to. It goes away tomorrow otherwise. The meeting notices will be thrown in the bin."

My whole body is shaking. How I want her to turn to me and say, "I know you meant well, lass. I loved your mother, and your grandfather was my father's best friend until the day he died. I'll think about it, I will, for their sake if nothing else."

But I know this is just a dream too far.

Her back to me once more she says quietly, "I'd be grateful if you could tell the bairn I'm off-colour so that's why I won't be able to watch her play today."

I want to ask her to forgive me and my blundering ways. I'd like to reach out and touch her shoulder. If I stretched out my arm I could … but I won't.

Instead, I go into the kitchen to put on my boots and coat to make my way to the football match. I see Lydia's paint pot and brush from yesterday drying on the windowsill. They're lying in wait for my daughter to create her next masterpiece which will adorn one of our walls. Dolly has three lined up already in a carefully positioned row on the side of her kitchen cabinet.

So, after all the blood, sweat and tears, I've still been sent away with a flea in my ear.

The silence coming from the other room as I let myself out is ringing in my ears … and now I don't know how it can ever stop.

Chapter 20

"I can't believe we finally won!" Lydia exclaims as we wander home from the match, "you were right Mr Ralph, it was well worth the wait."

The curls around her face are matted, and her ponytail is half in, half out of her bobble. She looks a perfect picture of happiness with her cheeks aglow.

"I'm chuffed for you both. You've worked so hard for a win, the whole team has," I say.

Ralph smiles down at Lydia and she looks up at him like the sun rises and sets on the top of his head.

"I only wish Mrs Dolly could have seen it, especially as it's the last match before Christmas," she says.

I was waiting for that little comment.

"I know, she'll be sorry she missed it. Hopefully, she'll be feeling better tomorrow."

"Yes, and then we'll be able to go and see her while you're at work and tell her all about it. I'm glad Mr Lockwood let you have the day off so you could see it, mum. It was the best moment of my life."

She sniffs, the cold weather making her nose run and I can't help but smile at her hyperbole.

Ralph looks at me, raising his eyebrows, the burning question sitting behind his eyes. I shake my head.

"Right, a hot shower beckons," he says, "well done, Miss Lydia, we've broken up for Christmas on a high note."

Lydia hugs him, and he gently tugs her tatty ponytail, telling her she needs to try out for England when she's older. I watch her almost skip inside the house to have her bath. Afterwards we'll drink hot chocolate while we run through the post-match analysis.

"Dolly knows everything," I say when Lydia's out of earshot, "it's not good, Ralph. She feels more than betrayed by both of us, but especially you. She wouldn't listen when I told her you only wanted the best for her."

He shrugs his shoulders, never fazed by much in life. Perhaps that's one of the perks of age.

"It's come out of nowhere, so she's bound to be shocked. Come on now, Hattie, don't look like you've lost a bob and found a tanner, it's not the end of the world. The worst that can happen is the town stays as it is and only a handful of us will be any the wiser. Nothing's signed so there would be no foul."

Oh, Ralph, I think, that's not the worst thing that could happen. That would be if Dolly never spoke to me again and cut ties with Lydia. I'd never forgive myself.

After Lydia goes to bed, I hear the back door go. I'm running on adrenaline because if I thought about it, I could tuck myself under the covers in bed and sleep for a week.

Ralph takes his shoes and coat off while I put the kettle on.

"Well, what happened?" I ask before he's even undone his top button.

"Hold your horses, let me get settled and I'll get you up to speed, such as it is."

I can hazard a guess what "such as it is" means. He heads into the front room while I make us a brew in double-quick time and take in through.

"Did you get in?" I ask as I'm sitting down, I can't possibly wait any longer.

The curtains are closed and the tree lit. Lydia has been busy writing Christmas cards and wrapping the gifts I brought with me way back in September. We've still plenty of preparation to do but making a start was a distraction at least. Under ordinary circumstances the house would be warm and snug, festive even, but that's a million miles from how I'm feeling right now.

"I did, but I had to knock a few times. I think the only reason she let me in was to give me a piece of her mind."

"What did she say?"

"More or less what she said to you earlier, I imagine. I wasn't expecting a welcoming committee and it's nothing I hadn't imagined her saying to me time and time again over the years."

He takes a swig of tea, resigned to his fate like the unflappable old soul that he is.

"Did she say what she wants to do?" I ask.

"Oh, yes, and then we chatted about the bright, shiny future of Wakeley for half an hour."

I see the twinkle in his eye.

"Oh, you," I say even managing a half-smile.

"Hattie my love, if you think for one minute Dolly Hunter will make her mind up in a hurry for anyone, you're more blinded by love than I thought. I only wanted to get the barrage over with sooner rather than later."

How I admire his mettle to face the wrath of our mutual friend and still be philosophical instead of crushed like I am.

"Did you tell her about Bernie waiting for her decision?"

"I did, and she said Bernie could get off his backside and go and talk to her if it was so important."

Oh, Dolly.

"I'll nip and see him tomorrow," I say.

Ralph puts his mug down, his eyes roaming my face.

"You look like you've been to war, lass."

"And that's exactly how I feel, Ralph. I'm riddled with regret about how I handled it, but more that I dragged you into it."

"I wouldn't change a thing," he says, "you've given meaning back to my life, you and the little lass. I was floating from day to day for too many years without even realising."

We sit looking at the tree a moment listening to the crackle and spit of the fire. My stomach starts to settle because what's done is done, I think. I'll do my best to make it right but that's in the hands of Dolly … and for another day.

"I'm going to put my tree up with Lydia tomorrow," Ralph says, eventually.

My head flies in his direction, but he still has his eye on my now infamous Christmas tree.

"Do you think that's wise, Ralph?" I ask.

He nods, his mind far away.

"Ay, I do," is all he says.

*

What on earth have I been thinking? I've been like a dog with a bone, wrapped up with the process far too long. The whole idea now seems like a ludicrous shot in the dark, some fanciful pipedream.

Ralph called for Lydia after lunch while I went to see Bernie to relay Dolly's instructions with a more polite choice of words. He'll probably be round at her house now.

I let myself in the back door of Ralph's and I can hear him and Lydia chatting as I'm taking off my things. It's bitterly cold outside and there's more snow on its way. I've never had the pleasure of a white Christmas before; I've always wished for one but the snow's either come early December and left too early, or in January.

"Mum, you made me jump," Lydia says, and Ralph also looks taken aback.

"Too busy having fun by the look of it, I see."

Ralph's new Christmas tree is already installed on a table in front of the window and half-dressed with baubles.

The lights are wrapped around ready to go on. I try and muster some excitement, so I don't ruin the atmosphere.

"That's looking a treat," I say, "don't you go making it look better than ours now, Mr Ralph."

"I fully intend to win the competition," he says, clearly enjoying himself, "I might have beaten you already because I've got tinsel. Christmas is a poor show without tinsel, don't you agree, Miss Lydia?"

"Mum doesn't like tinsel; she thinks it's old-fashioned."

My eyes round and I feel the need to rush to my own defence.

"I said I like it in other people's houses, Lydia, if you remember, but I prefer foliage for myself."

"Oh, you prefer foliage, do you?" Ralph mocks in a la-de-dah accent, "Anybody would think you're a bigwig from the city if they didn't know better."

I have to laugh, pushing him gently, and Lydia copies me.

She hangs a shiny, red apple bauble on the tree now, one from Ralph's new collection.

"I was going to ask Mrs Dolly to come and look at the tree when we've finished, but she's still a bit poorly," Lydia says, scanning the neat row of baubles waiting in line to be hung.

I catch Ralph's eye and he flashes me a reassuring smile.

It takes us another hour but when we've finished, we don our outdoor clothes and head down the front steps to look at our efforts from the prime position across the cobbled street. I try to perish the thought that Dolly might spot us.

"Mum, please will you put our tree lights on?" Lydia asks on the way down the path "They'll look lovely together."

Raising his eyebrows Ralph nods in encouragement, knowing all too well why I'm hesitating. What's the difference between one tree or two trees, I think as I switch our tree on. It's cold comfort; I only hope Ralph doesn't regret his bold move.

"Why are there candles everywhere?" Lydia asks crossing the road.

"Well, there was an accident at the copperworks, as it was called," Ralph points to the building on his left, "many, many years ago. I was only a young lad. Everyone lights a candle to remember it."

She mulls over this nugget of information a second or two.

"I think that's a nice thing to do," she says finally.

The three of us stand side by side in the darkness, Lydia in the middle. I want to enjoy the moment, but I can't help my eyes straying towards Dolly's house. Ralph nudges me, and I look back at the beautiful scene.

"I think ours is the best, Mr Ralph," Lydia says, "sorry to have to tell you, but I do."

"Oh, you do, do you, miss? You can fall out with people, you know," he says with a chuckle.

I'm happy when we head back inside, and not just because of Dolly. I feel the whole town's eyes on us.

Tonight, is choir practice which means Dolly is due to make an appearance, but I very much doubt it. Glancing at her house as we walk across the cobbles, I'm sure I spot her outline behind the curtain. Perhaps it's only my frazzled mind playing tricks on me.

"I think we should light a candle from now on, mum," Lydia says, as we close the door behind us.

"Yes, I think that would be nice."

My throat tightens at the sensitivity of my young daughter.

*

We set off early to choir practice as I need to organise refreshments in Dolly's absence.

I'm proud of the choir and the effort they've put into learning such technical carols when not one of them can read music. The improvement since we began rehearsals in September is impressive; what a shame if Dolly now misses out on the grand finale of the concert.

I'm filling the milk jug when I hear the latch on the church door go.

Lydia and I bob our heads out of the back room to see who it is, and my heart sinks when I see Dolly bustling down the aisle towards us, untwirling her scarf as she goes.

"Oh, am I glad to see you," Lydia says, rushing to greet her and almost throwing her arms around Dolly, "it's been so strange without you these last couple of days."

Dolly's face softens a little, but she only says, "Don't knock me off my feet, now," giving Lydia an awkward smile.

"Are you well enough to help out?" I ask her.

"I wouldn't be here if I wasn't," she says, resolutely avoiding eye contact, "I'll finish off while you set up."

She hangs up her coat up and gets straight to business as the frost settles itself around me yet again. That's as much as I'm getting, I think, but then that's as much as I generally get.

By the end of the session, I have new-found confidence we can put on a decent show on Christmas Eve. Knowing it was the last time to practice meant I had their full attention and commitment and afterwards we all shared a moment of quiet satisfaction together; come what may the team effort cannot be ignored.

We gather for refreshments for the last time and the choir split into their natural groups talking animatedly about the upcoming concert.

Joyce Pinner suddenly looks over at me from her little tribe of three and I catch her eye. I hold my breath under the spotlight.

"What's this I'm hearing about a council meeting, Harriet?" she asks loudly, though I'm barely a few steps away.

I cast a glance at Dolly who's thankfully preoccupied with Lydia.

"It's about the possibility of new jobs at *Lumley's* as I was explaining the other week," I say quietly, my eyes scurrying back and forth towards Dolly.

"Ah, right. Bernie mentioned something to Sally Evans at teatime, that's all and then she mentioned it to me."

I feel out of the loop and wish I'd had a chance to speak to Bernie. He's kept his powder dry all this time and now he's suddenly the village gossip. Joyce goes back to holding court and I start breathing again.

Lydia is busy giving Dolly chapter and verse about the football victory as we clear up.

"It sounds like I missed a cracking game," Dolly says when Lydia comes up for air.

"You did, it's a shame you weren't feeling well."

Now, I'm forced to replay the events in my mind, the events that prevented Dolly attending the match.

Locking up, I see the choir has regathered outside the church and I recognise the sheet of paper Phillip Croft is holding in his hand is the Council notice. There's a debate taking place about how many new jobs could be up for grabs. Bernie must have taken the opportunity to put the notices up when we were otherwise engaged. Good plan, if a little crafty on Bernie's part.

"Why now, I wonder though?" Phillip says, "It seems out of the blue. Come on, Harriet, do you know more than you're letting on?"

They all turn to me in unison. I can only shrug my shoulders and give them a tight smile.

"I suppose there's only one thing for it, folks, you'll just have to go along to the meeting and find out. It's not my place to tell you the council's business."

Dolly is looking decidedly po faced in the middle of the crowd.

"Night, everyone," I call over my shoulder, "are you walking back, Dolly?"

We usually take the short walk home together, so it will look odd if we don't tonight.

"It's alright, you go on without me," she calls, "I just need a word."

Oh dear, that sounds ominous, I think but I head off, holding hands with Lydia to walk past the candlelit houses.

As Lydia chats away, I have one thought racing around my head.

I might not be lucky enough to win the war but judging by the appearance of the council notices around town, it looks like I might just have won a battle.

Chapter 21

I want to go home.

I want to lock the door behind us, push my feet into my slippers and watch Lydia jump into her dad's arms. I want to hear her telling him of our adventures and the new friends she's made.

I want it then to be my turn to slip into the warm embrace of my husband and breathe in the comforting scent of him … of home. I want to hear him whisper in my ear, "We've missed you so much, but I couldn't be prouder of you, Hattie. There's nothing more you could have done, so move on now with the satisfaction that you did your best."

I want to climb the two flights of stairs to see grandpa sitting in his chair by the dormer window, tactfully keeping out of the way for a moment. I want to bend and kiss his forehead, lined from a lifetime of life, and feel his careworn hand on my cheek. I want it so badly…

But I want, never gets.

I need to tough it out. There's the small matter of the carol concert to get through.

I've answered untold questions since the planning meeting. The townsfolk obviously won't lay down to have their belly tickled without wanting to know chapter and verse about their future. There's a faint charge of excitement in the air, but these people are understandably wary when nothing much happened for years and now it's all happening.

Bernie told me Dolly didn't answer the door to him despite his best efforts, but he decided to see her silence as permission to proceed. He said she sat stony faced throughout the council meeting, listening to all the questions and answers, not giving anything away or talking much. This wasn't a surprise as these are classic Dolly behaviour traits at the best of times, and attending the meeting is still more than we could have hoped for. She didn't sit next to Ralph which raised quite a few eyebrows.

He's called every day and taken Lydia up to Dolly's house for a couple of hours. They all went to the church to do a Christmas clean together. Since then, I've been dressing it with foliage, masses of it.

Every time I think of a man building a little tin church so all his employees could have a place to congregate; somewhere of their very own. I can imagine it packed to the ginnels with families wearing their Sunday best, the children shuffling in their seats with boredom and their parents' disapproving glances.

Now, I'm grateful for it being my place of refuge for a couple of hours a day.

Ralph is coming for a Christmas tea tonight. We'll be too busy tomorrow with the concert and the general flurry Christmas Eve brings with it.

He's brought one of the Christmas cakes he made weeks ago with Dolly and Lydia for after our tea. He told me Dolly cooked them for hours in the range she still uses from time to time for hearty, homely things like stews and rice pudding. Sometimes he was lucky enough to have one left on his back step after a swift knock and a disappearing act.

That particular avenue of pleasure has been closed off by Dolly now, perhaps for good.

Although I'm keen to speak to her before Christmas, I've decided neutral territory might be the best option. The thought of knocking on her door again leaves me cold, so I've decided to pull her to one side after the concert to have a "chat" on the walk home. Ralph's going to take Lydia to his house for a while so we can be alone. This is the plan, but best laid plans can fail as I now know only too well.

"I think I'll make this a new tradition," Ralph says, polishing off his fresh bread and ham sandwich. There's tinned pears and cream for pudding to go with the cake. It makes me think of grandpa.

"Leave the plate, we're short," Lydia jokes just like grandpa would as she watches Ralph raking up every last crumb. She was clearly thinking grandpa too.

Ralph throws his head back laughing, making Lydia's eyes widen with surprise until she laughs along with him.

We've had plenty of fun these last months in between the tension. Ralph has a way of putting life into perspective with his straightforward attitude.

I wish I wasn't so sensitive but then Daniel says you can't have one without the other. My sensitivity may be a curse at times, but it's my driving force. He's more than happy to pootle through life.

I miss him terribly. I wanted him to come too but as he said, you can't run a kiosk if you're not there. He's been so good supporting my strange venture and especially in letting Lydia come with me. Thank goodness for Facetime is all I can say. Our daily videocalls have kept us together as a family and telling him the goings-on in Wakeley is the highlight of my day.

Ralph and I demonstrate our finely honed washing up routine after tea. We do it almost without thinking nowadays, having grown accustomed to each other. Our relationship is very easy; we talk if we want to, stay quiet if we don't. We're relaxed in each other's company, and I value it.

We settle down afterwards in our usual spots to watch Lydia finishing off the Christmas card she's been making for Dolly. It's a candle with a red, orange, and yellow tissue paper flame. She's gluing it onto a black background so, "It stands out better," she said. It was her own idea.

She holds it up for us to take look when she's finished. It's a clumsy, childish work of art with hidden meaning. My throat tightens.

"Simple yet effective," Ralph says, "always the best way."

I smile, grateful for the lightening of atmosphere. He has a way of doing that, yet he's completely unaware.

"Just a little greeting to write inside and then you're done. What are you going to say?" he asks her.

"I'm not sure yet; I'll have a think and finish it off tomorrow."

"Good idea," I say, "it's past your bedtime anyway, Miss Lydia."

She wraps her arms around Ralph's neck and gives him a kiss on his cheek. His face glows as he pats her arm. I think again of grandpa.

I still want to go home.

Ralph's sitting with a gift on his knee when I return. He's already restored his football table to give to Lydia for Christmas, so I'm not sure why he has it.

He offers the present to me, and I sit down and stare at the little package.

He clears his throat.

"While we have a quiet minute, I thought you might like one of these," he says.

The gift is clearly an awkward shape made to look more awkward by the way he's wrapped it. I imagine Ralph tousling with the wrapping paper so I'm at risk of being overcome and making a show of myself. Life in Wakeley is such a roller coaster ride.

I carefully peel the tape back at one end and peer down the gap.

"Well, I assume you're not using the paper again so just get it opened," he says.

I smile and tear the paper off then hold the gift by the handle to look at it. Ralph has given me the most charming little candleholder almost identical to the one he has burning in his window each night.

"I made one for my mother out of an offcut of copper pipe when I was an apprentice at *Worthies*. They said I could have it when they knew what I intended it for. I cut the pipe in half because it was so long, and I don't like waste, as you know, so I kept it in the shed. It took a bit of polishing after fifty years sitting in the damp, I can tell you. Well, anyway, I've had another go at making one and it's turned out alright … if you squint when you look at it."

"Alright?" I say my voice almost a whisper, "Ralph, it's the most thoughtful gift I've ever been given."

"Well, I wouldn't go that far, the handles a bit off."

I laugh and look at the copper pipe, polished to perfection, the bottom end of the circle nipped and bent outwards, then attached to a dark wooden base. I see the tiny brass screws holding it in place, and a copper handle, curled and attached to the side. It is "a bit off" which makes it all the more charming; perfectly imperfect, imperfectly perfect.

"Thank you," I say, "you know I'll treasure it, Ralph."

He nods, smiling coyly.

I light a candle from the dresser then place my gift centre stage in the window, admiring the glow of the copper against the flame. Ralph's thoughtful nature reminds me yet again why I've been so drawn to this place and the people who live here.

Now I reach deep into the branches of the tree, breathing in the wonderful smell of the sap.

I present my friend with a small black box. He shuffles in his seat, unsure what to do or say as I imagine it will have been a long time since Ralph has given and received a gift. Anyone would be out of practice.

"Don't look so worried, it won't go off, I promise," I say pushing the box a little nearer to him.

He takes it and pulls his glasses out of the top pocket of his shirt. I watch him as he reads the tag attached to the red bow.

"To Ralph," he mutters, "it would make us very happy if you accepted this gift. (Hattie had it repaired as she won't tell you). Merry Christmas my old friend. Yours, Robert."

Grandpa wrote the tag in July, sitting at the table with me while I was tapping away on my laptop, working on a case.

Ralph looks up at me, and then down at the box again, unsmiling. Lifting the lid slowly his eyebrows shoot upwards.

Restored to its former glory, my great grandfather's watch is gleaming, nestled in the black velvet. He shakes his head but doesn't move for a while as I watch him intently. I can almost feel his pleasure at receiving such a gift. Selfish act, unselfish act; whichever it may be, it won't stop me doing them if I can.

"You remember my grandpa's dad, George? Well, this is his watch. Grandpa said there's nobody else he'd like to wear it more, especially as you knew him. He has another one so this was just lying in its box, and he couldn't see the point. Grandpa meant what he wrote, Ralph, it would make both of us very happy if you accepted it."

He moves his forefinger over the old face of the watch, taking in every detail. It took a long time to find someone with the skills to fix it nowadays.

"Well, talk about *Tommy Top-it-up*, or whatever they call him, your gift has knocked my gift into a cocked hat."

I tell him not to be so daft, just as he would say to me. He takes the watch out of its box to get a closer look.

"I don't know if I dare wear it. I think I'll keep it for Sundays," he says, turning it over to read the insignia.

"Try it for size," I say.

He takes his old watch off and I reach across to fasten his new one for him. I'm pleased with the brown leather strap; it sets it off well.

As he twists his wrist this way and that, he looks every bit like the big kid he is who has just been handed a new toy. I think back to when Lydia gave him the advent calendar; it seems so long ago now.

"I'll ring your grandpa later to thank him. I was going to give him a call before Christmas anyway. Thanks, lass. I'll not have a Christmas to match this one again that's for sure."

"Of course, we will," I say, horrified at the thought.

We sit quietly watching the candle flickering in the window for a while before I dare to address the elephant in the room.

"Has Dolly said anything to you yet?"

I know the answer already, though I'm compelled to ask it every day.

"I don't know what I'd do without my daily grilling now," he smiles, "the answers the same as yesterday and the day before. If it wasn't for Lydia, I wouldn't be getting a foot in the door so thank goodness for small mercies, I say."

"I'm thinking of pulling her to one side after the concert tomorrow."

"You know, it might be best to wait. She'll not be rushed, and she might feel backed into a corner. I wouldn't want you to get your hand bitten off."

"I thought being outside might help. I'm losing my mind here Ralph, and I'm running out of time. If it's a 'no' from Dolly, then I'd rather deal with it."

What dealing with it will amount to, I haven't decided yet.

"What did you say to me all those years ago? Slow and steady wins the race, that was it. Be patient, Hattie, if you know what's good for you. You've waited this long, don't bugger it up now."

I sigh and turn the television on. He happens to be right, however I'm on a deadline.

"There's that black and white version of *A Christmas Carol* on at nine if you fancy it?" I ask, glad of a change of subject.

"The best one," he says as I head to pour him a whisky and myself a glass of port from the dresser. I bought the old sherry schooner glasses years ago. Ralph was impressed I cared so much about the appropriate receptacle as he called it, for my sherry. I carry the Christmas cake in with a hunk of cheese on each piece the way we like it. Ralph has banked the fire up and I draw the curtains before lighting the tree.

We snuggle back into our seats to await the start of the film. Ralph looks at his new watch from time to time and I stare into the flames. I glance up to see Dan's Christmas card along with grandpas on the mantle. I haven't had any from the town, but Ralph said this is normal and not to read anything into it. He knows now I read anything into everything, and he tells me it must be exhausting.

What a sad thought that Christmas has been forgotten completely by Dolly or hidden like a guilty pleasure by others for half a century.

As the music starts and the titles roll for the film, I think Ralph will be asleep in five minutes as per usual. We're wearing the poor man out between us, but I'd put a stop to it the minute I thought he wanted or needed me to.

Oh well, I think as I finish off my cake and tuck my woollen throw under my chin in anticipation of our favourite Christmas film, I've offered them all the pot of gold and it's sitting there waiting to be taken.

I remember it's Christmas Eve tomorrow. There's nothing more to be done tonight so I focus on the film and wait for the peace to descend.

Of course, I'm fooling myself. It doesn't take long to realise that peace is just as elusive tonight as it's always been.

Chapter 22

"Mum, you're brushing too hard," Lydia says.

My mind isn't on the job in hand as it should be.

"Sorry, love, I'm rushing. I just want us to get to church ahead of the choir to make sure everything is perfect."

"If it's not perfect now after the hours you've spent there, then I think you've had it."

She sounds like Ralph. I laugh as I finish off her ponytail with a dark green bow to match her tartan blouse.

"You look a Bobby Dazzler," I tell her, thinking of grandpa.

I remember the last time he said it to me. I was gliding down our grand staircase at home wearing my wedding dress and he was waiting at the bottom with a red rose buttonhole in the lapel of his navy suit. His hair was creamed and slicked back so much you could count the comb marks if you felt like you wanted to. I'd spent as long choosing his suit as my own dress because he was guest of honour at the tiny gathering in the parish church. Even though we sat on one side rather than two, we barely filled three rows. In the end, the intimacy made the day more special, and he had a little dream come true in walking me down the aisle.

The memory fades and I notice Lydia is looking me up and down.

"You look like him too," she says.

I've put my hair up and I'm wearing my cream woollen dress. My happy dress for happy days, I must keep reminding myself, even raising a smile attempting to trick my brain into releasing endorphins for a little stress relief. I discover it's a myth, at least it is today.

Dusk has descended but the candles haven't been lit yet, and the street is in the bluey haze of a snowy twilight. It's eerily quiet and I'm trying to shake off the sense of foreboding as I head into the woods, lantern in hand. I need it so I can see my way through the shadow of the trees, the darkness descending immediately as I turn off the road. Tapping the snow off our boots, I usher Lydia straight to the back room to make a start. Fifty candles are waiting to be lit to stand either side of the pathway and I've got fifty more to dot around the windows of the church. Ralph has lined the seats at the front for the choir, so I ask Lydia to place a crisp song sheet on each one while I set to work. They know the words well enough, but I know what nerves can do to someone. I want the candles in position before the vicar arrives as I'd like to surprise him too if I can. I check the foliage and tweak the flowers at the altar on our way outside.

Once the final candle is lit, Lydia and I stand and take in the scene, holding hands.

"It looks like a fairy princess cottage," she exclaims, her eyes sparkling like a kaleidoscope from the flames.

If that's the response from everyone who attends today, I think, I'll take it.

"Harriet Scott!" the vicar calls from the edge of the woods, "You have been busy!"

"My, my Lydia, you and your mum have done a splendid job. Splendid. It's a sight for sore eyes on a wintry day, indeed it is."

I follow him in, and soon the choir begins to arrive in dribs and drabs. We have our usual little vocal warm up session as we wait. I've brought along extra fan heaters so they can all wear just a white shirt and either black trousers or a skirt without freezing to death. They look the part, like a proper choir. I feel like a proud parent.

Ralph appears first in his best Sunday outfit, with a festive red tie. He smiles at me at the piano and sits alongside Lydia. She's swinging her legs on the far end of the front pew. Smiling up at him as he speaks, I can imagine Ralph telling her she looks like a proper lady or something along those lines.

I end rehearsals with ten minutes to go.

"Well, you'll be the talk of the town by the end of tonight, choir," I say fiddling with my sheets of music to keep my hands busy.

"Ay, but I'd rather not be singing to myself," Joyce says with a laugh, and the others join in. I laugh too, though I can't help but think that many a true word ...

Through the open doors I spot Bernie and Graham Lumley. They're with their wives and Graham's children heading down the woodland path. They're chatting away, pointing out the candles, and I'm warmed by the sight of my friends. I wave from my piano stool, and they wave back with a broad smile.

A couple of minutes later Sally and Ted Evans appear with three more people and then a steady stream of old and new faces arrive. Within five minutes the church is almost half full.

Part of me has been wondering if Dolly will turn up at all, however the saving grace I have is that I know she would never miss a church service.

She read my mind it seems, suddenly appearing with a small entourage, the familiar roll of my stomach signalling her arrival. Everyone greets Dolly like royalty on her way down the aisle and she nods towards me and the choir before making her way to sit on the far side of Lydia.

I incline my head as I take a sip of water, only too pleased to hide my face behind the glass.

Still people are arriving. The church is almost full now, with more still coming through the doors. I'm beginning to worry about fitting everybody in. Oh, the irony of people standing squashed together at the back of the room when only moments ago I was wondering if we'd have a turnout of any magnitude. Everyone is smartly dressed in seasonal outfits and animated chattering is floating around the church. I soak up the life in the room.

The noise level steadily decreases as the vicar stands on his well-worn spot at the altar. Eventually silence descends and I briefly bask in the glow of Ralph and

Lydia's smiles of encouragement. Dolly's eyes are fixed firmly on the vicar as he introduces the first carol to be sung by the recently formed *Wakeley Warblers*. Low laughter ripples around the congregation.

The choir stands and I hit the first note on the piano of a jolly sit up, sit down version of the *Twelve Days of Christmas*. They sound impressive, and other than Phillip Croft forgetting his *eight maids a milking* which raises another chuckle at his panic-stricken face, it turns out to be the perfect icebreaker. One down, two to go.

After the vicar expresses his gratitude for the record attendance and his Christmas reading, we sing *I Saw Three Ships*. This time I can safely say we earn the title of bona fide choir. I glance occasionally at the entranced congregation, Dolly included, taking note of the quality of the singing and the harmonies. The earnest expressions on the faces of the choir as they sing their heart out touches my heart and we exchange broad smiles as the final note is met with silence.

Reverend Burton clears his throat.

"Well, I think we can all appreciate how hard you've worked with Harriet to reach such a high standard of singing in such a short time," he says, his words laced with a touch of incredulity.

Just you wait, vicar, I think as he draws breath to begin the sermon.

"So, it's that time of year once again. A little different to other years I think we would all agree, but it feels like the church must have felt many years ago at Christmas."

I can't look at Dolly. My eyes fix firmly on Lydia who's twitching and shuffling with boredom, just the same as the children in Thomas Worthington's day.

"You know, I've had many conversations about bringing the church up to date. Change is inevitable in life, and we're supposed to embrace it. Perhaps we have no option, if not to embrace it, then to accept it if we are to survive. But change is rarely a welcome visitor."

He pauses to look around the new flock staring back at him before continuing. I imagine the pinched look on Dolly's face in my mind's eye.

"I like my life. I like getting up and having my first cup of tea in the morning, watching the birds while I have my toast, going into my warm, cosy study, thanks to Dolly," he smiles in her direction and she inclines her head, "and catching up with my correspondence before visiting the sick and the elderly and going home to a hearty tea with a glass of wine. Eventually I wander up to bed for a good night's sleep before I wake refreshed, ready to do it all again."

He smiles and looks around the church briefly and I can tell he's taking note of the change in atmosphere.

"But what I realise is that if the church is resistant to change, it doesn't matter what I think, there will be no flock for me to gather or to tend. Then there will be no job, no home, indeed no life I know and love so much.

So, when Harriet Scott knocked on my door and asked if she could form a choir, shamefully, my initial thought was, what's the point? No disrespect to the few of you who have always attended church, you are my friends, but you were few and far between. I was apathetic, thinking it a nice idea but a waste of time."

He pauses to smile my way.

"How wrong I turned out to be. The choir would have been deprived of the joy of rehearsals, giving the church a renewed sense of purpose. They wouldn't have started coming with their families to church on Sundays, which in turn encouraged others. But the worst thing by far is that we wouldn't have been able to experience the magic of today. We wouldn't have had the moving experience of seeing so many people from the town join together as one to celebrate Christmas Eve by candlelight in our magnificent church.

This year has been a memorable year for the town for good reasons and for bad. The point I am making to you all as I stand here this Christmas Eve is that change comes in all forms and often when we least expect it. But as today has proven, sometimes, just sometimes, the pleasure it brings has the ability to dull the pain, if not forever at least for a while.

I glance at Dolly who's holding hands with Lydia, staring at the vicar. Her face is pale, her expression strained, and the tears sting the back of my eyes because she'll think I've planned this with him and we're all still in cahoots behind her back. She'll never believe me when I tell her I'd no idea what he was going to say. I catch Ralph's eye and he purses his lips and drops his head in mock reprimand attempting to console me. The dear man is willing the tears welling in my eyes to stem. I look down at the piano, unable to muster a smile even for him for once.

How I want to go home.

"Well now, I've kept you from your families long enough," the vicar says, "the choir will sing us out but for now I just want to say, I'm expecting everyone every Sunday from now on and no excuses. In the meantime, I wish you all a very peaceful and happy Christmas."

As the congregation laughs at the vicar's little joke, I try to pull myself together for the last carol of the service. I heave a steadying breath and raise my head to face the choir and begin the bothersome *O Holy Night*. We nearly gave up many a time due to the complex harmonies.

Tonight though, I think we will all be united in feeling so glad that we didn't. It's by no means perfect, but the energy that surrounds us I know will stay with me always. The performance has 'soul', haunting me for so many reasons.

But most of all, it signifies the hard work we've done together over three months to try and sprinkle magic and joy on our fellow townsfolk.

When silence returns to the church, many are dabbing their eyes with handkerchiefs, others sitting with an expression of awe. I shiver when a tingling runs down my spine.

Magic and joy have arrived in Wakeley, just in time for Christmas.

"Merry Christmas," resounds around the church, as people turn to their neighbours to wish them true greetings of the season.

I head over to wish the same to the choir and tell them how delighted I am for all of us that it went so well.

"Merry Christmas, Miss Harriet, and a Happy New Year, you've filled our town with Christmas cheer," they all sing in perfect harmony.

I laugh with surprise, imagining them rehearsing the little ditty just for me.

As the choir disband reliving the experience already, I wander over to Lydia and Ralph just as Dolly is making a swift exit down the far side of the pew.

My eyes follow her all the way out of the door, then I give Lydia and Ralph a tight smile.

"Can I go with Mr Ralph to finish off my message on the Christmas card. It won't take long but I know what I want to write now," Lydia asks me.

"Of course, you two go and I'll tidy up here."

If I'm honest, it's a relief to have a chance to compose myself before I go to see Dolly.

"You did us proud, lass," Ralph says, "I thought the choir would be a right shambles, I can't deny it and I doubt I was alone."

"Oh, ye of little faith," I scold him as Lydia is leading him away by the hand.

Graham and his family are waiting around, and Bernie introduces me to some of his children and grandchildren.

Smiling at each other, Bernie slides his arm side on around his wife, Heather.

"It's been nice to give the family a reason to come to us this year, Harriet. We usually end up going to one of their houses for Christmas. We've had a good start already to the festivities," Bernie says.

I wish them many more.

The vicar makes his way over, shaking his head and beaming at me.

"That was some Christmas message," I tell him "But it's done me no favours with our Miss Hunter."

"What do you mean? Are you accusing me of stirring the pot, Miss Scott and me, a man of the cloth, and all?"

We share a laugh as he gathers his things to go home.

"Would you mind if I locked up and returned the keys to Ralph tonight? I would love to sit here alone a moment by candlelight."

"Of course, that's why it's here, Harriet."

He pats my shoulder as he strides out the door with his papers under his arm. I picture him on his way to a hearty tea and a glass of wine, watching his favourite Christmas shows before cocoa and a solid night's sleep. A man with no worldly worries.

I sit on the front pew where Lydia and Dolly sat holding hands together. My own beliefs are more spiritual than religious, but peace and tranquillity feed any soul. The heaters have only just been turned off, but it's colder now everybody has left. Perhaps it was the people who warmed it.

I know it's time for me to head up the road and talk to Dolly, I can't put it off any longer. Bite the bullet, Harriet Ann, I think, you're a big lass so get on with it.

Blowing out the last candle inside the church, I grab my lantern and head outside to do the same to the ones lining the woodland path. I fiddle with the old lock, the giant ornate key sticking partway. There's a technique to it I remember Ralph telling me.

A familiar voice appearing from the big silence startles me.

"Have you got a minute?" it says.

Spinning around I see Dolly standing on the path between the candles, her misty breath from the cold night, flying into the atmosphere. The sight of her is almost ethereal.

"I was just on my way to see you," I say.

"I thought you might be, but I just wanted a quick chat. Can we go inside?"

I notice suddenly that I have a strange sense of calm for the first time in Dolly's presence. Perhaps it's because I can't possibly make anything worse than it already is.

"Of course," I say, picking my lantern up by the handle to take inside.

As I close the door behind us, the temperature is now icier than outside. Dolly sits down on the back pew and nods to the space by her side. I pause, then place the lantern on the windowsill above us before joining her. The light hovers above her head.

I sit, eyes forward, staring at the altar now and waiting for her to begin. I have no intention of stealing her thunder when it appears she has her own agenda.

She takes a deep breath. How odd that Dolly should appear nervous after all these months of me being on the back foot.

"I suppose you think I've been hard on you," she says.

I sit perfectly still and unresponsive, mindful not to spoil her flow. She sniffs.

"I've been doing a lot of thinking of late, as you might imagine, more than I've done in nigh on forty years. You know plenty about me. You've read my letters, so you'll know all about my father and how much I missed him when he died. You'll know all about my stepfather and the upset he caused me and my mother. I'm sure Ralph will have filled in the blanks."

I turn my head to the right to look at her. The last sentence reminds me again how wrongly I've played my hand.

"But to me, you were just a stranger who rolled into town. You came under false pretences, good intentions or not and you went behind my back. You upended me, so my tidy, orderly way of life became unrecognisable."

I look down at my hands now, ashamed of her perception of me.

"I admit I was furious, but you got both barrels because I was even more so with Ralph for his deception. Soft lad or not, he's still always been my mainstay, somebody I trusted.

You'll find it funny; I know you will, but I thought he fancied you to begin with. I thought you'd been seeing each other, and it somehow reared a side to me I'd never experienced before, and I know now it was a jealous side. I had bad feelings towards my stepfather and stepsister, Ruth but it was never jealousy, more anger and resentment. The realisation about how I felt shook me."

My face drops, this was the last thing I was expecting her to disclose to me tonight.

"Don't look like that, I know it's ridiculous now but at the time I thought you were setting yourself up to be a cosy little family. You got on so well and you seemed so at ease with each other. I'm ashamed of the way I spoke to you and more so because you're Margaret's girl with a heart as golden as hers was. And the bairn, well…"

She hangs her head.

"I handled it all wrong, Dolly, it's my fault not yours."

"Perhaps we've both made a few mistakes between us.

I'm touched by her grace and instinctively lay my hand on top of hers briefly before I pull it away.

"Now, as my mother used to say, people come into your life for a reason, a season or a lifetime and I believe that. If I'm truthful, I've had more than a few sleepless nights over the years about the deprivation our town has endured. Smaller things, like the library, the Post Office, the pub, the park and bigger things like the school and *Worthington's*. I watched on as people died or moved away and it gradually became more and more like a ghost town to what it was. I'd become not exactly inured but accepting. As long as my little house was standing strong that's all that mattered."

She sighs saying, "But that was not the right attitude, I know it now."

"I could have told the town to keep Christmas again, but I never did. I can't lie, the pain lessened over the years, but I had a sense of pride that people supported me in the memory of my father. That was wrong too, selfish. We could have had what we'd had tonight years ago, but I allowed myself to wallow in it. I didn't know it then, but I did. Nobody from the town was ever going to challenge me and it would have gone on until the day I died. If I'd still had your mother, she would have put things in perspective, but she was gone."

She pauses and turns to me. "You know, if you ever want to know what she was like, look inside yourself and you'll find her."

Her bottom lip trembles slightly, and I can't bear it. I grab her hand and she places her free hand on top of mine. It's as though we're clinging to each other for a moment. I feel a tear drop from the end of my nose and Dolly rustles in her handbag. She hands me a tissue; such a small yet motherly gesture that touches my core. I realise I've never had a mother or even a mother-figure such as I can remember. Gran was too busy living in the spiritual world to mother me.

"I like the plans you've made, and I've given them my blessing, though I don't know who crowned me Queen of Wakeley. I think they're well thought through and more importantly, I think they'll work. Well, most of them, perhaps the museum idea can go on the back burner until I'm gone. I'm not so keen on droves of tourists piling out of coaches with sweaty sandwiches in their backpacks, gawping in my window."

We share our first laugh together. It's like the release of a valve, the tension flies out of me, and every muscle relaxes.

"Dolly Hunter saves Christmas," I say, laughter still in my voice, "it sounds like the title of a book."

She smiles at me, and I see what mum saw for the very first time. I see the *real* Dolly Hunter.

"It's bloody freezing in here, sorry god," she says, raising her eyes upwards, "come on, lass lets go get the bairn and soft lad and have a sherry."

I grab my lantern again and take the church key from my pocket. I need to hurry and get locked up so we can start this Christmas Eve.

"Hang on a minute, there's something I want to show you, Dolly says, "I know Ralph said the entrance light was unfixable for the time being, but it was a white lie. I didn't want you to see what we'd done until now."

She switches on the light from the inside and points to one side of the church door.

What can she mean? I've read the plaque dozens of times on my way in and out of church.

In memory of Eric Hunter who died saving the lives of hundreds of men in the copperworks fire of 15th December 1973.
There is no greater love than this: that a person would lay down his life for the sake of his friends.

As I come to the end with a lump in my throat, my eyes drop to a new brass plaque below it. Freshly mounted and shining my way in the candlelight it reads:

And grateful recognition of his best friend, Robert Hargreaves, for his own selfless actions in saving the lives of his friends and colleagues.

Dolly is smiling proudly at me when I finish the sentence.

I read it again, tears now welling in my eyes. I think of Ralph's verdict on the plaque as simple yet effective. He might be wrong for once; simple yet profound might be a more apt on this occasion.

"Ralph and I organised the plaque between us," she answers my unspoken question, "I should have thought of doing it years ago, you're not the only one with regrets."

Our smiles tell each other we have reached an understanding.

I take a photograph of the plaque with my phone to show grandpa, then we blow the candles out between us and set off down the path. The snow is packed underfoot so we take our time, carefully placing each step so we don't slip.

Turning into the road I notice it's brighter than when I set off. I look up, my eyes blinking to focus on the brightness.

The streets are brighter because every inhabited house now has a tree twinkling in the window. The curtains are pulled back to display row after row of Christmas wonderment. I gasp and put a hand to my mouth.

Dolly is grinning all over her face at me.

"You're haven't got the monopoly on pulling a plan together, you know," she says.

The town hall at the top of the road is strung with lights and there's a tree twinkling on the top step. Even the broken houses have fairy lights draped across the front. My eyes are everywhere, soaking up the sight. A sight that's symbolic of a town's new-found hope.

Our house is lit up, and so are Ralph's and Mrs Turrell's. We walk nearer and I see even Dolly's house has been "festivicated" as grandpa calls it.

Ralph and Lydia are waiting for us at the gate, as they've been witnessing my reaction along with everyone else. There are people hanging out of their front doors clapping and singing *"We Wish you a Merry Christmas,"* at the top of their voices.

A powerful feeling rises in me, taking me a moment to recognise it. Joy, that's the only way to describe it, pure unbridled joy.

The light is blinding after the long years of darkness.

"We had another town meeting after the planning meeting," Dolly says as we reach Ralph and Lydia at the gate, "there's a lot been going on behind closed doors on your behalf."

She pauses and looks deep into my eyes. "It's the least we could do, Hattie."

Oh, the pleasure of my name coming from the mouth of Dolly Hunter.

I wipe a tear and nudge Ralph, saying, "You, mister, you're devious you are."

"What, I can't help it if I can keep a secret, can I? I kept yours for long enough, I reckoned it was only fair Dolly had a turn."

We laugh and join in the singing. All the while I'm thinking how swiftly life can change, for the worse but also for the better.

I spot the candles, still burning brightly in the windows as they have for forty-nine Christmases before. They demonstrate how the old and the new traditions can blend seamlessly.

Steadily, everyone returns to the warmth of their houses to enjoy their Christmas.

"Merry Christmas," Dolly says to Mrs Turrell, and we chime in.

"Merry Christmas to you too, Dolly," she says, "and to all of you."

Alongside Ralph, I think what a huge part she had to play in getting Dolly and her mother's life back on track.

"Be with you in a second," I say, "I'll see you inside."

Once I'm in our house, I grab another small box from the deep branches of the tree, breathing in its scent as I did only yesterday. Today I'm a different person; one who is lifted, lighter.

I weave my way back to Dolly's and when I'm inside I think about the last time I stood in this house. Lydia's pulling her boots off, and Ralph has gone through to stoke the fire. It doesn't take much encouragement to come back to life. Dolly pulls two sherry schooners and another glass out of the dresser along with the sherry bottle. I admire the tiny glass with the handle and a Scotsman in a kilt.

"I haven't had this out in a long time," she says, handing it to me.

Lydia settles down with her milk and chocolate cake looking like she lives here. Ralph's looking at his sherry like he'd rather be looking at a whisky. We wait for Dolly to sit down in her chair by the fire.

"So, merry Christmas, and to many more," she says raising her glass. We raise ours together and Lydia does the same with her milk.

I follow Dolly's eyes to the tree with the white branches. The style is back in vogue, having come full circle and I can tell the baubles are the same ones she will have hung when she was a girl. It must have been so moving for her trimming it after so long. I'm pleased she at least held on to it.

"Do you remember how your tree was the first one up by a country mile, Dolly?" Ralph laughs.

I hold my breath, hoping he hasn't dampened her mood at the memory.

"Of course, I do, Ralph Kellett," she says, "I'm not senile yet!"

Flashing him a cheeky little smile she gets up from her chair to head over to the dresser on the back wall. She pulls out a gift, wrapped in robin-covered Christmas paper.

"This isn't valuable in monetary terms, but it is in other ways," she tells me, "It's for both of you."

Lydia sits at the side of me on the settee and carefully unwraps the gift. Inside is an old-style advent calendar displaying a cosy cottage with a Christmas tree in the garden. Lydia opens the flap of number one to show a candle in the window, then looks at me smiling.

"It's a bit late for this year, I know but you'll have it for other years," Dolly says.

She sits by the fire and tells us the story of two best friends at Christmastime and the reason the calendar is so precious. I hang on to every word of it, we all do, as Dolly drifts back into the happiest time of her life. She's so absorbed with the tale I think she forgets that we're here.

Even Lydia is quiet when she finishes the tale. I look at Ralph and he has tears in his eyes the same as me. The story will be as new to him as it is us, and he'll have his own memories of that time. I know not all of them are happy ones.

"Well, I don't know about everyone else, but I've had a belly-full of sentimentality for one day," Dolly says, and the mood is lightened with humour once more.

She and Ralph think they have so much to thank me for, but I have learnt so much from them, I shall forever be in their debt.

Ralph disappears into the kitchen and returns with Lydia's card in his hand.

"You nearly forgot this," he says.

Lydia takes the card to hand to Dolly who pulls it from the envelope, her eyes scanning the card. She manages to wipe away a tear so quickly I wouldn't have noticed if I wasn't paying attention.

"I've written something inside. Read it out please, Mrs Dolly, I've had a bit of help with the spelling," she says.

Dolly takes a breath.

"To Mrs Dolly, merry Christmas, lots of love from Lydia," she reads, adding, "nice writing. Thanks for looking after me and for coming to watch football every week in the cold. I am glad you got some wellies."

Dolly chuckles, thanking Lydia and displaying it on her mantle. She turns to Ralph.

"Looks like we had the same idea," she says reaching for an envelope behind the clock.

Ralphs pulls his card out which has a crayon drawing of him kicking a football.

"To Mr Ralph, merry Christmas, lots of love from Lydia." he reads, "Thanks for looking after me and for playing football every week. I was glad when you sent Jake off for un-sportsmanlike behaviour when he said girls in goal are crap."

The rest of us burst out laughing, as Lydia says in all seriousness, "Well, it was cool."

I spot a brief glance between Dolly and Ralph.

"Well, I'll leave you to it, if you don't mind," I say, "it's almost Lydia's bedtime and we need to eat and get ready for Santa coming."

Back in Dolly's kitchen I discreetly take the box and card from my pocket and put it behind the kettle while they're preoccupied with Lydia and her preparation for Santa's visit. I can't face giving my gift to Dolly and I know what she'll say when I do.

"I can't take this, lass," I can hear the words in my mind, "it's yours, it's not right."

I put the note with it because I thought I might have to drop it through the letterbox. Only a short while ago I had my doubts that I would ever set foot in this house again.

I think it will be better for her to read the card alone. She'll understand how much it means to me for her to have mum's eternity ring dad bought her on their first

265

anniversary. I glance at my mum's wedding and engagement ring twinkling away on my hand. This way we both have a piece of her with us all the time.

"Thank you, both," I say, "merry Christmas, I wish for everything you wish for yourselves."

They return the greeting then smile at Lydia who's already hugged them in turn and jumped with the fearlessness of a child from the step into the snow. We wave as we go down the path through Dolly Hunter's back gate.

The last thing I see is Miss Dolly and Mr Ralph looking at each other as they close the door to us.

Chapter 23

Lydia and I eat our tea by the fire and sit for a while chatting about our plans for tomorrow. I can feel the old excitement building now my mission is accomplished. I'm finally calmed, carefree even because I can see the wood for the trees. After fifty years, next year will be the year to end all years.

Christmas, and all it has to offer now languishes before us.

We've checked the website that tracks Santa's Christmas Eve journey and discovered he's already in France, so we decide we must get a move on. The last thing my daughter and I do together this unforgettable night is to put a mince pie, a glass of sherry and carrot for Santa and Rudolph on a plate on the hearth.

My adrenaline is flagging and I'm keen to get to bed myself, but I have presents to bring downstairs and I want to bring Daniel and grandpa up to speed.

By ten thirty the fire has burned low. I place the guard over, turn the lights out on the tree then last but not least, blow out the candle.

I peer up and down the street through the window, watching the snow in front of the woods glistening in the moonlight. I finally have my white Christmas. The town is deserted, and the wonderful silence wraps itself around me.

There's an envelope waiting for me on the mat by the front door as head to go upstairs and I grab it to take with me to open in bed.

Lydia is sleeping soundly in gran and grandpa's old room. As I turn off her lamp, I think of how Christmas came and went almost like any other day for them.

My bedroom is cosy but unfussy, just the way I like it; in normal life, I find it conducive to a peaceful night's sleep. Pulling up the covers I hold the envelope in my hand and stare at it intrigued.

"To Hattie," it says, and I immediately recognise the writing.

Inside is a card with a drawing of a star shining in the night sky on the front. How tasteful it is, I think. As I open the card, a letter falls onto the duvet, but I read the card first.

To Hattie and Lydia, wishing you a Merry Christmas and a Happy New Year. Love from Mrs Dolly, it reads, *P.S. Hattie, I think you should have this to add to your collection.*

As the words sink in, I think about today and all that has happened between two women. How I should have known all would be well because after all, Dolly is still the Dolly my mother knew. She was always in there.

I open the folded letter and see a tiny sprig of yellow roses printed at the top of the page. I put it to my nose and breathe the scent of the paper. I close my eyes briefly and swallow before I begin reading:

My dear Dolly,

I was so pleased to hear about your promotion at Lumley's. That's two in one year! You'll be running the place before long at this rate. I bet your mam is so proud of you and the extra money will come in handy.

I'm glad you put in a good word for Ralph to work there too as I often think of him and how he used to make us laugh. He was always so popular at school, and I quite liked him myself for a while if you remember. I can't believe we never found out where he disappeared to for all those months.

Life sounds so much better for you nowadays and I'm glad things settled down in the end after all the upset.

Well, Dolly, I write with some news. I don't think it will go down too well due to the circumstances but rest assured, I'm very happy about it. It's been a bit of a surprise for Ronnie and me, but I'm going to have a baby.

I know, like Ronnie and mam and dad too, you'll be worried about me, but you mustn't, Dolly. I'm sensible as you know, so I've weighed up all the risks but there's also something inside me telling me to go ahead and have this baby. I'm not concerned in the way I know you will be. It's the right thing to do for me and for Ronnie. I'm having the baby for me, but I get the feeling he'd love a family even though he'd never say, bless him.

Mam has come around a bit and she's started knitting. I've got enough cardies and bootees to set up a stall and I love getting them out of the drawer to look at. I've picked the wallpaper for the baby's room already. It's yellow with tiny grey rabbits hopping all over it. I've got the material to make curtains to match too.

I know you will have your reservations but please be happy for me, Dolly. I hate to think of you fretting about me.

All I know is I love this baby already. It's so strange how you can love a person who you have never even met.

Sorry to give you a shock but I'll look forward to your next letter, they always make me think fondly of you and of Wakeley.

Your loving friend,
Margaret xx

I put the letter to my nose again after I've finished reading. It has a combination of scents; special scents of two special women: My mother and Dolly Hunter.

I place the letter in my top draw with my locket and close the drawer. Then I prop the card under the lamp, turn my pillow over and snuggle down under the covers.

Strangely, I'm not tearful as I would have imagined. Instead, a sense of peace washes over me as I drift off to sleep with my mother's words floating around my mind.

How she loved me.

I'm so tired. I've been planning the future of Wakeley for literally half my life I suddenly realise.

So, that Christmas Eve I slept the soundest night's sleep I'd had since I was seventeen years old.

I thought perhaps I might have earned it.

Chapter 24
Dolly Now

I can't lie, I'm ready to put my feet up; I've been at it all morning and I'm shattered.

The turkey has been cooking in the range since well before first light and I did the potatoes and vegetables last night before bed because there wasn't a cat in hells chance of me sleeping with all the excitement of the day.

I've had a look at the Christmas pudding cooking instructions on the cellophane wrapper. It will just have to steam for an hour and a half as I haven't got a microwave and I've managed well enough without one until now.

We've decided to spoil ourselves and eat Christmas dinner on a tray by the fire. We had a pleasant morning opening gifts and eating sausage sandwiches to put us on until dinnertime and now Ralph has gone home to get changed. I've given the house a once over. I've not gone mad, but it is Christmas Day and like my mother used to say, a house should sparkle on Christmas Day.

I take another peep at Margaret's glamorous ring with the cluster of diamonds in a heart shape. I don't know if it goes so well with the yellow duster in my hand, but I've promised Hattie that I'll wear it. I didn't make a fuss about it because she had already explained in her letter why it was so important to her for me to have it ... and to wear it.

She never mentioned me giving her the last letter her mother sent me either and I was glad about that. I just felt it was only right she had it and some things are better left unsaid.

Life's a funny old game; it's almost like I've got a piece of Margaret back with me after all these years of missing her.

I'd better catch my breath this Christmas as I doubt my feet will touch the ground next year. I've told Bernie that I'll be on the planning committee, and I admit I'm quite looking forward to it. I hope planning will be passed because we're stuck without it, but I see no reason why it wouldn't be. There's enough land around *Lumley's* and no objections up to now.

I'm not a fool, I know it won't happen overnight, but it needs to happen. It took me long enough, but I just needed a push in the right direction. I can't help but feel bad about putting Hattie through the wringer these last weeks. Anyway, we've reached an understanding, so I'll not dwell on it and send myself round the twist.

My eyes wander to the tree as I sit down and wait for Ralph to arrive. I remember how I used to sit looking at it for hours with my mother years ago. I did the same last night with a sherry before I went to bed, and I raised a glass to her.

We'd sit with just the tree lights on, and dad would moan, "It's like the black hole of Calcutta in here," when he came home, then switch on the lamp. He said it every time and he laughed every time. I've no idea where Calcutta is even to this day, and I doubt he did either.

I wonder now if my mother wanted to keep Christmas again like I did. We never spoke about it but perhaps we didn't want to upset each other by bringing it up. If you leave things too long, they do one of two things, stay the same or fester, but they never get any better.

"That's ancient history, Dolly," I say to myself, "Onwards and upwards for you now."

I'm startled out of my thoughts by a knock on the door. I fluff my hair in the mirror over the mantle and think briefly about how the makeover's done wonders for me if I do say so myself. I don't pile the makeup on as the bairn did, but a little more doesn't do any harm. I need to faff about with my hair a bit more often, but I have to say it's worth it. I feel a bit more confident somehow; I've got a bit more sass as my mother would have said.

I open the door to see Ralph on the bottom step with a bottle of white wine in one hand and a bunch of flowers from Sally Evans's in the other. He must have bought them yesterday as today is one of the only two days she closes all year. His hair is damp and combed back and he has a tie on under his red V-necked jumper.

"Come on in, you'll catch your death with wet hair in this weather," I say, ushering him inside, "would it have killed you to rub a towel over it before you came out?"

He shakes his head and smiles, no doubt thinking he should be getting some toffee from me for turning up with wine and flowers.

I thank him as he hands me his gifts. It's a nice gesture mind, and I'm glad now I've got a little something under the tree to give him after dinner.

In the silence of the street, I hear a van trundling towards us as I'm closing the door. I lean outside and put one foot on the top step to watch it pass slowly by.

I know who it is, but I can't see them for the falling snow and the tall shadow of the houses on the windscreen. I can picture them both well enough though, strapped in the front and waving like mad.

I raise my hand with the flowers still clutched within it and grin, watching the van then until it's out of sight.

A reason, a season or a lifetime suddenly springs to mind as I close the door to celebrate my first Christmas with Ralph Kellett.

Well, Margaret, your girls came to me for a reason and a season. Now they've appeared in my life, you can rest easy my dear, sweet friend.

I'll make sure I look after them for you ... for the rest of my lifetime at least.

Printed in Great Britain
by Amazon